Clara L Matéaux

Woodland Romances

Or Fables and Fancies

Clara L Matéaux

Woodland Romances
Or Fables and Fancies

ISBN/EAN: 9783744792981

Printed in Europe, USA, Canada, Australia, Japan

Cover: Foto ©Andreas Hilbeck / pixelio.de

More available books at **www.hansebooks.com**

THE CORMORANT AND THE FISHES (*see p.* 160).

WOODLAND ROMANCES;

OR,

FABLES AND FANCIES.

BY

C. L. MATÉAUX,

Author of " Home Chat," " Around and About Old England," &c.

SIXTH THOUSAND.

CASSELL, PETTER, GALPIN & CO.:

LONDON, PARIS & NEW YORK.

CONTENTS.

CONTENTS.

WOODLAND
ROMANCES.

WOODLAND ROMANCES.

THE RIVALS.

"I WOULD rather be my lady's hawk,
    And perch upon her hand,
Than I would be the deerhound grim,
    To range this forest-land!"

"I would rather be my lady's
    hound,
And lie low at her feet,
Than I would be the falcon proud,
    Her careless glance to meet!"

"I would rather be the Marlyon
    rare
She holds by silken guide,
Than I would be the greyhound
    tall
    That wanders by her side!"

"I would rather be the trusted
    friend,
    Led by one glance of love,

Than I would be the falcon fair
    She holds—but on her glove!"

"I would rather be her priceless
    bird,
    With jesses all of gold,
For many a tale of heron slain
    My falconer hath told!"

"I would rather be—just what I
    am—
    An old dog, tried and true,
Than a mere haughty, selfish
    thing—
A toy, Sir Hawk—like you!"

EAGLE AND CROW.

AN eagle, with its mighty wings outspread,
    Once, in the broad glare of a summer's day,
Swooped down upon a lamb, and from the flock
    He bore it straight away:
The bird had mighty claws, like traps of steel,
And safely winged off with his helpless meal.

A raven watched, and saw with great surprise
The stolen lamb ascending to the skies:
"Why should not *I* fly down and take a sheep—
    Poor is the watch they keep;

I'll choose a large one, fit for many a meal:
As well a sheep as lamb, if one must steal.

    " I'll clutch him as the eagle did, with ease,
    And bear him to my nest amid the trees."
    Down flopped old raven, but the tangled fleece
Caught his thin claws, nor could he them release
Before the shepherd loosed them in a rage,
And put the sable prisoner in a cage,

Then, mocking at his fluttering, wild distress,
Cried, "My fine fellow, you should aim at less,
And learn that what an eagle dares to do
Can be no lesson for weak folks like you."

THE BATTLE OF THE
FROGS AND MICE.

THE frogs had decided
    Again and again
That they would be masters
    O'er each swamp and plain;
But the field-mice objected,
    They would not submit,
And each side did wonders
    Of courage and wit.

More fierce grew the struggle,
   And desperate deeds
Took place in the shadow
   Of willow and weeds ;
To end all the turmoil,
   And worry, and woe,
The brave King of Frogland
   Soon challenged the foe.

He sent off a herald
   The message to take,
And warned him to hurry
   O'er briar and brake.

'Twas a toad in a tabard
   All decked out with green ;
At the rate that he went at
   It scarcely was seen.

The mice were all busy
   In council that day ;
But they looked up and mocked
   As Sir Toad came that way.
He stopped, and bowed gravely,
   Not heeding their rage,
And challenged their leaders
   With his to engage.

He drew out a broad leaf,
   On which was the crest—
His master's sign-manual,
   A frog's thumb-impressed.

"This agreement is legal,
   As all mice can see,
And shall be held binding
   On them as on me.

"I defy them with rushes
   To fight to the death,
Or at least till both parties
   Are quite out of breath—
Till one or the other
   Shall humbly deem fit
Himself and his army
   To yield and submit.

"I call on each leader
   His standard to drop,
When this wearisome question
   Has come to a stop;
The crown, for the future,
   Quite settled to be
On the side that is winner.
   Signed, F. R. O. G."

The challenge accepted,
   The herald hopped back,
And joyous the hopes
   That he left on his track;

For mice were nigh tired
  Of war's dreadful din;
Besides, they all fancied
  Their side sure to win.

Oh, mighty the stir,
  And loud was the boast
With which each great leader
  Encouraged his host!
King Frog signalled thousands
  From river and fen,
While Mousey the valiant
  Called up his brown men.

The morning rose stormy,
  And red was the sky,
When met the brave armies,
  To do—or to die!
And sharp the long rushes
  They bore o'er the field,
And loud rose the war-cry,
  "We never will yield!"

Oh, would I could picture
  The glorious sight,
When army met army
  In desperate fight!

When many a
field-mouse
Was borne to
the ground,
When scarce-
ly a froggie
Unwounded
was found !

They battled so
bravely
That late in the
day
Still found them
engaged
In the same
horrid fray !

Nor yet had their fierceness
With sunset gone down,
Nor yet was decided
The fate of the crown,

When, high o'er the clamour
  Of squeak and the croak
Of mousie and froggie,
  A fearful sound broke!
And, ere they could manage
  To scamper away,
A dreadful thing happened
  To finish the fray!—

Some owls, grim and hungry,
  Swooped down in a trice,
And caught up the poor frightened
  Froggies and mice!
That settled the question
  For ever and aye,
For they swallowed both armies,
  And then flew away!

THE BURIED SEEDS.

A LITTLE maiden blithely
   Flung in the earth some seeds,
She did not know what they might be—
   Fruit, or flower, or weeds;
She thought she heard a whisper,
   She bent her golden head,
When, much to her amazement,
   These were the words they said :—

"We're sad and very sorry
   To leave the sunlight sweet,
To lie deep-hidden from all eyes,
   Pressed down by careless feet.
What can we do but wither,
   What can we do but die,
In earth, where mortals lay their heads
   When life has flitted by."

The tiny maiden's eyelids
   Filled with unbidden tears,
She put her warm lips to the ground,
   And tried to soothe their fears—
"Rest quiet, little seedlets,
   I've heard my father say
That, though in earth our forms are laid,
   They live again one day."

Winter followed summer,
   Dark, and so icy cold,
Snow falling thick like veil of white,
   Bitter the breezes rolled.

The child thought of the voices
  That she had heard repine,
And often stooped to listen,
  But now they gave no sign.

Then spring again came, breathing
  A sweetness o'er the earth,
And slowly, with a struggle,
  It chased the winter's dearth ;
It tore the veil asunder,
  It scatter'd far the snow,
And all fair things, long hidden,
  Began again to grow.

Once more the sunshine lighted
  The maiden to the place
Where she had laid her golden head,
  And whisper'd words of grace.
Soft flushed her rosy dimpled cheek,
  She clapped her hands with glee
There, struggling from their hiding-place,
  Tall slender stems to see.

" Oh, welcome, flowerets, to the light
  Of life so sweet and fair !
I knew One hidden from our sight
  Had made you all His care:
Nothing so humble, small, or weak,
  That His eye cannot see—
A bird, a bud, a hidden seed,
  A little child like me."

CONTENT AND DISCONTENT.

WHERE merry waters tumbled
  All gaily in the brook,
Where floating leaflets, tangled,
  All tried to peep and look;
Tried to see old Baldfin,
  The hermit of the cave,
Hidden 'neath some crevice,
  Or floating grim and grave.

Around him sudden splashing,
  Out darted little fish,
As full of fun and frolic
  As kindly heart could wish.
Came Glitterside the pretty,
  And Silverscale the bright,
Finlet, with the scarlet stripes,
  Then Fluttertail in white.

All were so free and happy,
  While Baldfin, sad and lone,
For ever at life grumbling,
  Hid in his cave of stone;
Dreading some hidden danger,
  Some fisher, rod, or fly,
Or hungry heron, watching,
  With beak sharp-set and sly.

One day, all in a hurry,
  He came, with sudden splash,
Up where two pretty troutlets
  Were rising with a dash;
"My friends, I bring you notice,
  Contemn it not, 'tis true,
A water-spirit's coming,
  That means much good to do.

" To teach you, thoughtless brothers,
  How badly used are fish,
The fate that man awards them,
  To lie upon a dish ;
While other creatures fly above,
  Or roam the earth so sweet,
We are condemned below
  These waves to dash and beat.

"What have fish done, I wonder,
  That they should be debarred
From all which others find so
    sweet,
  I vow it is too hard;
The spirit that I own for friend
  Has other teachings, too,
And when you've heard him, I
    am sure
  You'll own great cause for rue."

"I tell you what," said Troutlet,
  To gentle Silverscale,
"That strange old Baldfin always
  Is on the fret and wail;
He sees no light in sunshine,
  Hears no music in the wave,
And has no praises for the life
  The great Creator gave.

"For ever is he dreading
  That evil must be near,
Forgetting present happiness
  In vain mistrust and fear;
Brother, let us be watchful,
  The spirit that he meant
Must be that one, most hateful,—
  Uneasy Discontent."

"He comes! he comes!" cried
    Baldfin,
  "Pray take him to your heart!"
"Not so," cried wise young
    Troutlet,
  Lest we might never part."
Away the two went splashing,
  They lingered but to say,
"We wish you, Mr. Grumbler,
  A very kind good-day."

MASKS AND FACES.

A GAY party of mummers, a strolling lot,
Lingered to rest in a shady spot.

Some soon fell asleep in the cool, pleasant grove,
The forest paths tempted others to rove;

They left all their robes and a fine tinsel
    crown,
Little thinking of thieves so far from town.

Yet a robber came and opened the box—
That creature of mischief, a dark brown fox.

He fumbled about all the properties fine ;
Nothing there seemed in Sir Foxy's line,

Till he came to the cast of a handsome face,
A big brave mask, full of sweetness and grace.

He cried, all enrapt, "Oh, how soft, yet clever,
This beautiful face, and it changes never!

"'Twere a fine prize to own, for its tender smile
Doth to sudden love my poor heart beguile;

"And besides all its beauty, a charm I see
In face so earnestly looking at me."

Long, long he gazed, and much he admired,
Until of that smile he grew somewhat tired,

For it never varied, but beam'd just as sweet
At snakes that hissed by the green retreat;

As it looked at a lark, that, darting by,
Carried its orison up to the sky.

It smiled alike at sunshine or shower,
Smiling till smiles had lost all their power;

Till fox turned away, he was ever wise,
The love-light passed from his nut-brown eyes,

As he thought, " Mere beauty, like cloudlets above,
Pleasant to look at are nothing to love.

"Yon's a wondrous mask, but when that is all said
There remains a smile and an empty head."

He cried, as he dashed through the tangled wood,
" I would not possess that fair face if I could."

THE TWO PATHS.

RESTING beneath a hawthorn bush,
   In the fair month of May,
I learnt a lesson from a bird
   Perched on yon poplar grey.

I knew the meaning of each note
   She twittered in the tree,
Bidding her pretty nestlings rise—
   Her fluffy one, two, three.

"Come, my brave baby birdies, come,
   Try how you all can fly,
Or you will never, never know
   The way up to the sky.

" See, I am waiting on this branch,
   High in the poplar tree ;
Try now, and stretch your pretty wings—
   Fly darlings, fly to me."

They stirred about, and flutter'd,
   Their tiny hearts a-beat,
Yet scarcely dared attempt to hop
   From out the safe retreat.

She called them, still so softly,
  "Don't hurry, sweets, or fear,
From one twig to another
  The road is very clear.

"Mind, Callow, dear, a broken
    branch;
  Why, Downie flies the best!
Don't chirrup, loves, until you're
    safe,
  Then you shall chirp and rest."

So slowly upwards, one by one,
  They came with careful hop,
And, breathless all, soon by her
    side
  They perched on that tree-top.

"Now look, my precious little ones,
  The two paths you may see,
One leading up to heaven so
    bright,
  Through cloudland, fair and
    free.

"The other takes us earthward
    down,
  A pleasant vision too,
Where golden corn and berries red
  Are growing, dears, for you.

"When you are faint and hun-
    gered,
  Needing to rest or eat,
Then use the short road, birdies,
  That lies beneath your feet.

"But when each happy heart
  . would soar
From danger, care, or wrong,

Then, children, take the upward
    path,
  And bear to heaven your song.

"Fly upwards oft, my darlings
    three,
  For skyward is the best,
And ne'er heed though some
    brothers vain
  Should mock at its sweet rest.

"Fret not that other birdies may
  Have stronger wings to rise,
Our praises, children, may ascend
  Beyond theirs to the skies.

"The Father, He that fashionèd
  Lark, linnet, eagle, you,
Full well knows if your life's aim is
  As earnest and as true.

"Remember mother's warning
    voice,
  On this your first day's flight,
For even tiny birdies dear
  Should know the wrong from
    right.

"Though earthward you must
    sometimes drop,
  Never upon it rest,
Arise with heart, and song, and
    voice,
  The skyward way is best."

Beneath a rosy hawthorn bush,
  In the fair month of May,
I learnt a lesson from a bird,
  Perched on yon tree-top grey.

'WHY?"

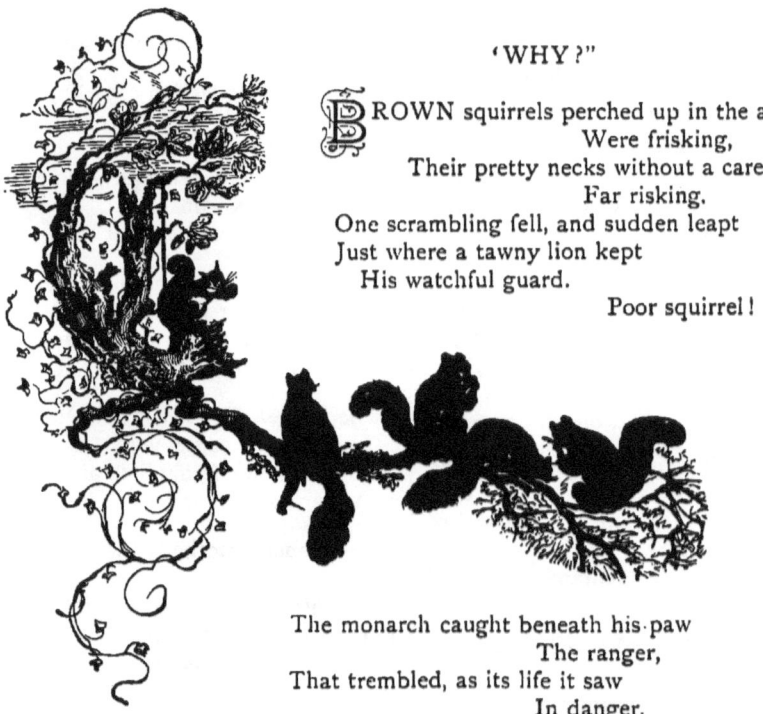

BROWN squirrels perched up in the air
                    Were frisking,
        Their pretty necks without a care
                    Far risking.
One scrambling fell, and sudden leapt
Just where a tawny lion kept
        His watchful guard.
                    Poor squirrel!

The monarch caught beneath his paw
                    The ranger,
    That trembled, as its life it saw
                    In danger.

"Oh, let me go!" it loud implored;
"Life is so sweet, great woodland lord,
    So very sweet
                    To squirrels."

The lion, having lately fed
                    Upon a kid,
Nodded its huge and shaggy head,
                    And mildly bid

The small new-comer, all a-flurry,
Tell him how, free from care and worry,
  In woodland homes
                    Lived squirrels.

" Oft have I watched them from this place
                    Antic and play—
A merry-hearted frolic race
                    By dawn or day ;
Whilst I, a lion, proud and strong,
Find the dull hours drag slow along,
  Lonely and sad.
                    I, squirrel,

" For ever on my guard must be,
                    And dread the light,
Lest wary hunters watch for me,
                    With weapons bright ;
The men who greet you with a smile,
If I but roar, will run a mile,
  Or try to slay ;
                    Now, squirrel,

Just give me, ere I let you free,
                    The real reason
Why you and yours can happy be,
                    Whate'er the season ;
All seem to have much work to do—
Are busy the long autumn through
  Among the nuts.
                    Tell, squirrel,

Why you, a tiny, helpless thing,
                    Small as my paw,
And I, great Afric's forest king,
                    Knowing no law ;
You, busy toiling all the day,
I, only seeking for my prey,
  Yet envying
                    E'en squirrels."

Wee Brownie begged the lion he
      Would let him go—
" Then can I answer fair and free
      All that I know ;
The one who tells a truth so bold,
Higher than he who hears it told
   Should safely stand."
                Wise squirrel !

The lion, curious, let him hop.
         In a twinkling
He sprang, as of escape he got
       Slight inkling,
Safe on a branch ; he stretched each limb,
Trying if it could safely cling.
   " Quite wonderful,"
             Thought squirrel.

" Your majesty has spared poor me—
       I am grateful :
To break one's word, I quite agree,
       It were hateful ;
So listen while I try to tell
How 'tis we pass our time so well
   And happily,"
          Cried squirrel.

" With every mate and brother
          We freely feed;
Yet as freely help each other
          In hour of need;
While lions hold it not a sin
To fight with and destroy their kin
  And nearest friends,
          Say squirrels.

" Ours is a simple busy life,
          As all may see ;
Loving each other, free from strife,
          Most happy we—
Living without the wish or will
To work the weakest creature ill—
  Mere harmless things
          Are squirrels.

" If I may hint it to your highness,
          So bold and strong,
Your race somewhat inclines to slyness
          And doing wrong :
That may account, none will deny,
Why at your roar all creatures fly
  In trembling awe,"
          Urged squirrel.

" Ill deeds bring fear, and fear brings care—
          That hateful thing,
Which darkens all the world so fair,
          As wise birds sing.
Cruel your deeds, expect to meet
Cruel reward ; revenge is sweet,
  So mankind say,
          Not squirrels."

THE BENT BOW.

A SAGE, in old Athenian times
  Most famous, once was seen
With children playing, on all-fours
  Prancing along the green.
"What!" cried a friend, "and can you joke
And frolic with such foolish folk?"

Up rose the sage, and seized his bow,
    But not to fight—
He only meant to show that he
    Was in the right.
The bow unstrung he laid before
    The mocking wight,
And cried, "There, sir, your answer lies
    Upon the floor.

"What, shake your head! And yet 'tis plain,
    For all agree
A bow kept tightly strung will soon
    Quite useless be;
So it is with the mind of man—
    It rest requires;
If ever on the stretch, at last
    It sadly tires."

THE LATEST NEWS.

PERCHED high on the
    branch of an elder tree,
    Loudly an old cock crew,
The common rang with his
    clarion notes,
    "A-doo-a-doodle a-do!"
Up ran a fox, "Oh, sir, step down;
Such glorious news has come from town!
Foxes and poultry have sworn a peace—
We are friends for ever, ducks, cocks, and
    geese.

"So come from the top of this
    elder tree,
  Come down, my feathery brother;
I feel a tender respect for you
  I have never known for another.

Come, let us embrace, friend, for under the sun
No more mischief will ever be done—
Hares will come on long visits, and even the mice
Will all love each other—oh, won't it be nice!"

"Indeed," said the cock, holding fast to his tree,
 "Excuse me, good sir, if I crow;
There's a fine pack of hounds coming yonder, I see,
 And surely they all ought to know:
Just stay to inform them of these your fine news."
"No," said the cheater; "I hope they'll excuse,
But I'd rather not meet them." Like lightning he flew,
Pursued by a loud, mocking "Doodle-a-do."

THE MOUNTAIN SPRING.

DRIP, drip, came down the water cool
  From a crevice 'mid hawthorn pink ;
Drip, drip, it fell in the little pool
  Where a child bent down to drink.
    He lifted up his fair, fresh face,
    And whispered as a sort of grace,
    "You pretty pool, low at my feet,
    I thank you for your waters sweet."

Rippled the pool, in tender
tones—
"Nay, thank me not, my
dear," it said;
"I am but just a little pool,
By mountain springlet fed,
That fills me, so I good may do—
Cheer thirsty birds, or boys like you."
"Then I the springlet and the pool
Alike must thank for waters cool."

"Nay," whispered then the
falling drops,
"The springlet's fed by
dew and rain:
That we alone no good could do,
My darling child, 'tis plain."
"Then thank you all—pool, stream, and
shower—
That kindly help boy, bird, and flower."
And then he would·have turned away,
But that he heard the driplets say—

"Stop, child! for all in vain we work
   To stay your thirst, my dear,
Did not the sun, so warm and bright,
   Send heat and radiance clear.
You owe it to his kindly face
That we drip cool in this hot place."
"Then," said the child, "my thanks are due
To the great sun as well as you."

The sun beamed down from mountain-top,
   Gilding each lily flower:
"Not mine to fill this rippling pool—
   They over-rate my power.
The pleasant draught the mosses keep
I caught up from the ocean deep:
The rolling ocean, fair and free,
Deserves thy praise far more than me."

Then, as the child began to thank
   The shining deep blue waves,
"Nay, nay, we do but work His will
   Whom all the world obeys.
Look up! look up! above us all
He dwells, that filled the pool so small,
Who made sea, land, all, by His nod.
Wouldst know His name? 'Tis Father—God!"

The child, still kneeling, raised his eyes
   To where the sky, so blue,
Looked down upon the dripping pool,
   Reflecting back its hue.
He softly clasped his dimpled hands,
And cried, "Pool, spring, and sun, and sea,
I thank you; but our Father kind,
Who made them all, I worship Thee!"

THE GREY WOLF'S MISTAKE.

YON huge grey wolf, the people's dread, a robber of the fold,
Thought, "I'll go seek the elephant—he's big, and strong, and bold.

" Such tender-hearted foolish thing 'twere well to have for friend ;
Shepherds will show less fear of me if I on him attend."

He wandered through the forest paths, searching with haggard stare,
Until he spied the mighty thing splashing by river fair.

It took of him but little note, except to turn away ;
" Good morning, sir," the grey wolf said ; " a lovely summer's day."

But as no answer he received, only a doubtful stare,
He urged, " I hope you don't believe what's said of wolves down there.

" They libel us most dreadfully, who never yet did ill,
That never slyly hid to spring, would not a rabbit kill.

" In fact, our fault, if fault we have, is being far too quiet,
Musing in our lone dens all day while other creatures riot.

" Those stories about wolf and sheep, good sir, are naught but fable :
We help the weak, protect the old, whenever we are able.

" I heard that you were strong and good, and handsome, that I see :
I should so like us to be friends ; kind elephant, agree."

He spoke in low and whining
    tones as elephant came
    near,
Not yet convinced. "What
    sign of ill dost see about
    me, dear?"

"I see two jaws with crim-
    son dyed, and spots upon
    your coat."
"Oh, yes," the wolf replied,
    confused, "a lamb flew at
    my throat."

"I see that coat all mangled, torn; how came it in such state?"
"Alas, some shepherd's dog, by chance, went wandering too late.

"I tried to show him on his way; he bit—who could oppose?
Dear elephant, when we are friends you'll guard me from such foes."

"Go hence and hide thy craven head," cried elephant, irate;
"How dare such mean and cruel thing to me of friendship prate!

"Seeking the shelter of my strength that you more wrong may do,
With fair false tongue and cruel heart: away, or you shall rue.

"*I* lend that strength or my good name to screen a rogue from harm!"
He raised his trunk with angry curl. It acted like a charm:

Off ran grey wolf with frighted growl, crouching by stone or rock;
Half mad with shame and coward dread before that honest mock.

At length he paused, and breathless cried, "Who fears your rage or
    power?
An elephant's no friend for me." Perhaps "the grapes were sour."

RATHER TOO CLEVER.

ONCE there raged a battle
  Between each beast and bird,
Such a noise and rattle
  Never had been heard.
In the morning early,
  The bat must join a side ;
Be he bird or beastie,
  Neither could decide.
So he fluttered both ways,
  Watching which would win,
Thinking that the safest
  To claim as kith and kin.
First, the fur-clad party
  Seemed to head the strife,
Then he cried, " Good cousins,
  For you I'll risk my life ;

Every one who sees me
  Says I am a mouse—
They among the animals
  Are well known in the house."
While he yet was boasting,
  Fortune took a turn ;
Victorious grew the birdies,
  As the bat did learn.
" Here am I, my brothers,
  Spying on the foe ;
They saw my wings, and took me
  For a bird, you know."
While the false bat talked thus,
  An old blue-coated jay
Cried, " Out, double-dealer,
  Hide you from the day ;

Nothing honest in you,
Ready either way:
Help from such were odious,
Keep you from our fray."
By-and-by, both armies
Swore a solemn truce—
They really found that fighting
Was of little use;
The brown bat, too cunning
Either side to own,
Now was left to wander
Unnoticed and alone;
Neither beast nor birdie,
He flutters in the air—

Oft at night we see him
In the twilight fair.
But no welcome stranger,
Travellers agree,
Is the broad-winged ranger,
Flying o'er the lea:
Harbinger of tempest,
Forerunner of storm,
Coming with eve's shadows,
Flying ere the morn;
Beasts will not come near him,
Birds, they fly away—
All such folk hate traitors,
So the fables say.

TRUE MUSIC.

A LITTLE lark went singing,
    Singing in the sky,

Bearing notes of gladness
    To the heavens high.

Trilling, trilling, trilling,
    Of the joys of earth,

Of its nest deep hidden,
    Of its mate's sweet worth;

Of the glowing roses,
  Of the daisy flower,
Of the wild wood posies,
  Of the summer shower.

Singing, singing, singing,
  Who knows what or why
Sings a happy little lark,
  While rising in the sky?

Near the hedgerow lowly,
  Far beneath its feet,
Gazed a poor old woodman,
  Toiling in green retreat.

"Oh," he sighed, all sadly,
  "Why should I be here,
While a lark goes singing
  Up in the skies so clear?

"Surely 'tis a hardship
  Birds may rise so high,
While we can but wonder
  And watch them as they fly.

"I've heard wise folk say
  All have work to do—
Some, perhaps, yet, happy lark,
  There seems no work for you."

Spoke a listening girlie,
  Such a wee bright thing,
" I am glad that birdie
  Can fly up there and sing.

" I am glad to fancy,
  As its hymns arise,

That our hearts go with it
  Far singing to the skies."

Right, my little maiden;
  Yon old man was wrong :
Birdie *had* his work to do,
  Although that work was song.

Not to all is given
  To raise so sweet a voice,
Yet to all is granted
  To hear it and rejoice.

Not to all is given
  To fashion thus their prayer,
Yet good thoughts can rise to
      heaven,
  And turn to music there.

THE TALE-BEARER.

LION and his mate one day
    Were chatting both together,
  Talking of this thing and of that—
      Their cubs, their court, the weather—
  When Fox came near, and whispered, " Sire,
  Something I've heard will raise your ire :—

" Sir Neddy Longears slightingly
    Speaks of your greatness every day ;
  He holds your majesty's loud roar
    No better than his bray,

Though Tiger, Leopard, Lynx, all
   own
Your title to the forest throne.

"He boldly scorns to call you royal,
And wonders I can be so loyal.
All this, and more.　I have been thinking,
Perhaps the creature has been drinking ;
He took me for a friend, 'tis true,
Nor knew me intimate with you.

"But I come of an ancient race,
True servants to your woodland grace ;
I——"　"Stop !" cried the lion, rising proudly ;
"Do not proclaim yourself so loudly.
As to Sir Longears, let that pass ;
What care I, though a simple ass

"May hold me lightly ?　*His* opinion
Is'nought ; but thou, false-hearted minion,
Who, with a meek and flattering voice,
Can in false calumny rejoice,
Beware lest I in haste should rend
The traitor who betrays his friend !"

THE FAIRIES.

THE fairies, the sweet fairies,
　　Have they *all* passed away?
Or do they yet steal out at night,
　　'Neath harebells blue to play?
To light the glowworm's tiny lamp,
　　That flickers after dark,
And safely guides lone wanderers'
　　　steps
　　With its bright elfin spark?

The fairies, the sweet fairies,
　　Say, have they passed away?
I love to dream of Mab's light
　　　throng
　　Making the shadows gay;
Of laughing Puck, who softly flew
　　Upon the night-bat's wing,
To stop the sports, that all might
　　　hear
　　Sweet Philomela sing.

The fairies, the sweet fairies,
　　Came, when the moon was out,
To hold their revels merrily;
　　All joined the woodland rout.

On mushroom broad their banquet spread,
  Red daisies each a seat,
Tall forests of the braken fern
  Their safe and sure retreat.

They drank fresh dew from acorn cups,
  They fed on honey sweet,
They danced so lightly that the grass
  Ne'er bent beneath their feet.
And when the joyous feast was done,
  Off hastened every fay—
So story tells—some good to do
  In its sweet simple way.

The weary milkmaid's pails they
    scoured,
  The sickly babe they rocked,
All good folks helped, unseen, unknown,
  While idle ones they mocked ;
The heedless sluggard pinched and
    tossed,
  The miser robbed of gold ;
But best they loved the infant's cot,
  And brought them joys untold.

Children could see the dreamland elves
  With clear untroubled eyes,

Nor ever mocked their wondrous
   powers,
   Nor thought them aught but
      wise ;
They never doubted, never feared,
   But loved the very name :
What youthful heart that hath not
      felt
   The power of fairy fame ?

Nay, do not call these dreams of
      mine
   Mere fancies for a child ;
I trust, to many a tender thought
   Such fancies have beguiled,
For they contain a truth sublime,
   Your scholar's lore above—
Its lesson, that the tiniest thing
   Hath power to work and love.

HIS LORDSHIP THE BEAR.

OME list to a tale that in Russia I heard,
'Tis the tale of a bear, and I'll own it absurd ;
Yet I think you will laugh at my hero in brown,
And the style that he once travelled into a town.
When he saw a fine sledge flying past where he lay,
"Here's a chance," thought Sir Bruin, "I'll go the same way."

The boy in the sledge was afraid of a bear,
And very much startled at seeing one there ;
He hallo'd and called, the far echoes rang back
The shouts, till Sir Bruin was close on his track,

And at last, with a leap like a huge furry wedge,
Plumped in 'twixt the lad and the back of the sledge.

With a groan of dismay the poor driver rolled out
On the snow, and lay there, almost smothered, no doubt ;

But the bear kept his place, while the horses raced light,
Reins flying, bells jingling, eyes red with affright.
"Now this," thought old Bruin, "is as it should be—
No more slow, cold walks through the forest for me.

"How fine 'tis to have these three creatures to run,
As swift in their flight as a ball from a gun!
I shall travel at ease now, and evermore ride,
Rolled up in these warm rugs I find by my side.
A thought, I will wrap myself up while I can,
Then if hunters *should* spy, why, they'll think I'm a man."

He dragged at the rugs with his great furry toes,
And managed to get them right up to his nose,
So that nothing was seen but his little red eyes,
And his muffled-up self of remarkable size ;
Ting-a-ring went the silver bells, galloped the three,
And soon in the distance a village they see.

Ting-a-ring, ting-a-ring, the people rush out—
" Hurrah, the new master !"—they raise such a shout ;
Ting-a-ring, ting-a-ring—eager hands the sledge stop,
While low bows and curtseys the humble folk drop ;
" Your greatness is welcome ; each one is your slave ;
Will you please to alight ?"—here a hundred caps wave.

Then stepped forth the bailiff, who spoke for them all :
" The banquet preparing is in the Town Hall,
But here in my mansion, sir, if you should deign
To rest for a time, a repast is spread, plain,
But the best in my power ; I am sure that your grace
Will excuse all mistakes in this out-o'-way place."

Sir Bruin felt queer, yet in those days of fable
To hide all such feelings Sir Bruin was able ;
While he drew up his wrappers far over his head,
And stepped from the sledge ere the last man had said ;
But he thought to himself, if he only got clear
This once, ne'er again would he come riding here.

He bent to the crowd (for soon found was his plot),
And murmured a something, they did not catch what ;
Then, gracefully stooping, leant on his host's arm,
As though, faint and weary, its offer did charm :
He walked as one tired, his tones, too, were low ;
But then, the great lord he was muffled up so.

They could see in that half light the brown of his beard,
He coughed as though really his voice must be cleared,
While he pressed to the chamber his host pointed out,
Making one hurried sign to disperse all the rout ;
Then passed in alone, closed the door with a bang,
While cheers and hurrahs for the new master rang.

They had not expected his highness just yet,
So there was a scramble each thing right to set ;
Some rushing with banners, some dashing with dishes,
Some placing the dainties—meat, pudding, and fishes—
Some shouting, some laughing, some decking the wall,
So busy were all men in Rostoff's Town Hall.

The musicians, fetched from their tea in a hurry,
Took a place in the background, all breathless with flurry ;
Big trumpet, brass cornet, triangle, and flute,
With a huge concertina, one half of it mute,
Began all out of time, with a roll of small drums,
An air we have heard—"See, the Conqueror comes."

Yet they need not have hurried, it seemed, for the guest,
Having chosen so soon at the bailiff's to rest,
Still was sweetly reposing, a fact his fat host
Announced in a voice full of dignified boast ;
So, of course, all must wait till it was his high pleasure
To join in the banquet prepared for his leisure.

They waited, and listened, and lingered so long,
That folks grew quite tired, and things went all wrong ;
The music sneaked off, and the cook vowed 'twas plain
The turtle would have to be warmed up again ;
The peas overdone, the potatoes gone wrong,
And his fine tender ducklings not worth a song.

They went to the bailiff's, and listened in vain—
His highness still slumbered, that one thing seemed plain ;
They waited two hours, then three, and then four,
They made odd little noises outside his room door—
Sneezed, coughed, dropped a chair, made a puppy-dog bark,
For by this time, you know, it had grown very dark.

One whispered, " Knock boldly, his slumbers must break,
And if he seems cross, say you knocked by mistake."
" I knock, sir! Oh, no, sir! not I, sir! not I!
Ever taught from my youth to let sleeping dogs lie ;
I have heard that some princes ne'er travel without—
And are apt to be rash in the use of—the knout."

That word quite explained all this worry and fuss
To wake up a stranger, 'tis not so with us ;
But *this* stranger, a lord of the old Russian fashion,
Might chain or might lash, if he felt in a passion ;
His dark muffled face and hoarse voice both did tend
To make each man present afraid to offend.

At last a new-comer suggested to peep
Through the key-hole, and see how he looked when asleep.
The bailiff pushed forward, and bent low his head,
Then breathlessly peered for his eider-down bed.
Around all stood silent, and stared as the man
Drew back, rubbed his eyes, and again tried to scan.

Up he sprang—" The bed's empty! our guest must be ill ;
That accounts for his keeping so silent and still."
He turned the brass handle, flung open the door.
Like their eyes, it wide opened, though nothing it saw,
For the large room was vacant, the table was cleared,
Of the fruit and old wine not a vestige appeared.

They stared at the couch, at the stove, at the chair,
At the ceilings and pictures, as though he were there;
Then they rushed to the wide-open lattice, and, lo!
Saw the marks of their visitor's footsteps below—
A bundle of rugs scattered wide here and there
Were the only remains of his lordship the bear.

Here was something to make the poor Russians turn pale,
For they knew not one end of the terrible tale;
They stared, puzzled, wondered, till, quite out of breath,
The sledge-boy come limping in, tired to death;
Yet he laughed as he said, "Never trust muffled face,
'Tis no sign that an honest one hides in its place."

THE SELFISH ONE.

TWO little birdies, in vest of brown,
    Came flying merrily over the down;
And, as they flew, they heard a song
That cheered them as they passed along—
                'T was "Cuckoo! cuckoo!"

One brown bird twittered, "Sweetest wife,
Where shall we pass our summer's life?"
She answered, "Choose, love; it to me
Must happy prove if shared with thee!"
                "Cuckoo! cuckoo!"

At length our wanderers built a nest
In greenwood-tree, as they thought best—
Built it of mosses, feathers, hair,
And filled it with five eggs so fair.
                "Cuckoo! cuckoo!"

And many a bird, that pleasant spring,
Thrilled the old tree with merry ring;
All chattering gaily as they flew
About their houses so snug and new.
                "Cuckoo! cuckoo!"

The handsome birdie that sang that song
Was idle as the day was long ;
She never seemed to do a thing
But in the skies to fly and sing,
          "Cuckoo! cuckoo!"

And yet it grieved our brown bird's heart
To watch their neighbours scream and dart ;
Wildly chirping, as though in danger,
If near a nest came the friendless stranger—
          "Cuckoo! cuckoo!"

They noted soon that her flight grew slow,
Her head down hung, as though 'shamed and low :
" Poor thing! let us ask her to stay and rest,
If she be weary, in our snug nest.
          "Cuckoo! cuckoo!"

" I do not think she will linger long,
And, Dickie, love, cheer her with a song."
"If you do, you'll repent, my little darling !
She is selfish and idle," cried a starling.
          "Cuckoo! cuckoo!"

" Idle and selfish ; that's the reason
We dread her visit every season.
'T is well to be kind, but not well to be
Friends with *all* birds we meet on a tree ! "
          "Cuckoo! cuckoo!"

Away he flew.   Dick said, " Poor fellow,
He is old, and fancies all leaves are yellow !
Go, birdie wife, so kind and sweet,
Invite the stranger to our retreat."
" Cuckoo ! cuckoo ! "

She instantly came, as for a race,
Fussily settled in mother bird's place ;
" Idle and selfish," the echoes still stirred,
Kind little hosts would not seem to have heard.
" Cuckoo ! cuckoo ! "

Birdie wife, from a maple-tree near,
Cried, " You are welcome to rest, my dear ;
We are sorry to see you lonely roam,
It must be so sad not to have a home ! "
" Cuckoo ! cuckoo ! "

" A home, and eggs or fledglings to keep—
To watch the eggs chip, and the young ones peep."
She stopped, but the stranger no answer
made ;
Perhaps she was shy, or, maybe, afraid.
" Cuckoo ! cuckoo ! "

" Sing a song, Dickie."   Dickie-
bird sang—
Notes where all welcoming kind-
ness rang ;
But the stranger only
stared from the
nest :
" Idle and selfish ! "—
the starling knew
best.
" Cuckoo ! cuckoo ! "

She rested long—she rested all day;
The little brown pair wished her safe away;
At last, off she flew, without saying good-bye;
Little brown mother was ready to cry.
                    "Cuckoo! cuckoo!"

Quickly she came down, anxious and light;
Turning her eggs, as she oft did at night,
" Why, Dickie, darling, as I am alive,
Six eggs are here, and we only had *five!* "
                    "Cuckoo! cuckoo!"

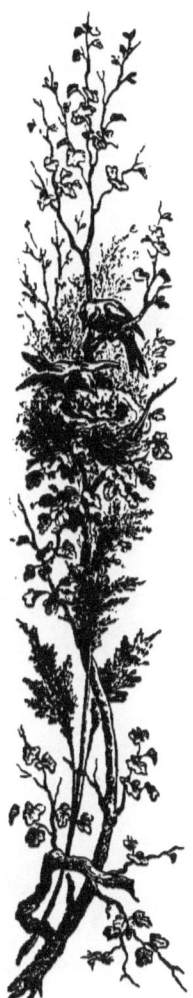

" Wife," said Dick as he yawned, quite hoarse,
" If six eggs there are, there were six eggs, of course!
Make room for me!"—" Why, it *is* quite a squeeze!"
Both the small parents thought, ill at their case.
                    "Cuckoo! cuckoo!"

Five eggs were hatched; then, from the other,
Soon came a wide-mouthed, ugly brother—
They, small and fluffy; he, big and bare,
With a hollow beak and a greedy stare!
                    "Cuckoo! cuckoo!"

Five, and this other; no, only *four!*
Odd! they had really fancied one more;
But the last-comer spread so in the way,
And, strangely enough, soon began to say—
                    "Cuckoo! cuckoo!"

He grew so fast, one could scarcely see
How tightly were packed the other three.
" *Four*, Dickie!"—" I tell you there are but *three*,
And the nest still as full as a nest can be!"
                    "Cuckoo! cuckoo!"

This one ever ready, with din loud heard,
To snatch tit-bits from each baby-bird;

E

The brown birds chirped, as for food they sped,
"A very fine child! but he must be fed."
                 "Cuckoo! cuckoo!"

They might not linger the loss to rue,
When in the nest they spied but *two!*
For, though they flew from morn till night,
These two sons' wants employed them quite.
                 "Cuckoo! cuckoo!"

But *one* at last!—there seemed but one,
Though he filled the nest as the five had done!
Where were those five? In his way, no doubt,
Selfish and strong, he had tumbled them out!
                 "Cuckoo! cuckoo!"

"Give—give to me!" was all his cry;
"I—I—I am starving! and wait, I—I——"
So eagerly snapping, that once, be it said,
He almost bit off Father Dickie-bird's head!
                 "Cuckoo! cuckoo!"

'T is ever the same. When the cry is heard
Of "I—I—I——," be it boy or bird
That says it, or sings it, or acts it, beware,
For a cold, hard heart is most likely there—
             Think of "Cuckoo! cuckoo!"

THE BUTTERFLY.

WHERE the sweet woodbine tangled
 About the hawthorn red,
Where the pale wild rose blossomed
 Above the violet bed,
Where glowed the purple mallows,
 Where hid the birdie's nest,
There flew a bright-winged butterfly,
 In richest crimson dressed.

Came near an idle schoolboy,
 So light of heart and eye,
He saw the happy insect thing,
 Dashing all lightly by;
Away he ran, pursuing,
 Off, cap in hand, he flew,
Crushing the pink-tipped daisies,
 The eye-brights azure blue.

Now on a berry resting,
 Now hid in rose so sweet,
Now fluttering gaily near his hand,
 Now dropping at his feet;
Above, below it darted,
 And then flew mocking by;
On ran the child, intent to catch
 The pretty giddy fly.

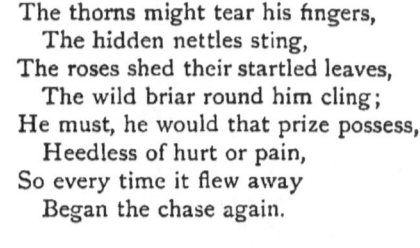

The thorns might tear his fingers,
   The hidden nettles sting,
The roses shed their startled leaves,
   The wild briar round him cling;
He must, he would that prize possess,
   Heedless of hurt or pain,
So every time it flew away
   Began the chase again.

At last he thought, all weary,
   The creature he must miss;
The pretty fly stooped low, and staid
   A violet sweet to kiss;
A rush, a crush, the boy at last
   Has caught it—waves it high.
Caught what? Alas! his hand but holds
   A broken butterfly.

DANGER.

"IF dangers we too closely heed,
   'Tis ten to one they come indeed."

Artful old Foxy made a vow
To lure the turkeys from yon bough,
Where safe they nestle greenly bright,
Like emeralds in the tropic light;
Such handsome birds, not like those seen
Gabbling about our village green,
But bright-plumed, radiant, and fair,
Like monster fire-flies hov'ring there.

" I long to capture one or more ;
But how ? " mused Foxy. " True, they're near,
Yet safe so far, no cause for fear
Have they, if only all agree
Not to descend from yonder tree.
My wiles are vain, yet cunning's strong :
These timid folk, expecting wrong,
I'll worry, threaten, make believe—
Their foolish fears may tempt them leave
The shelter which protects
   them now :
I cannot reach the lowest
   bough."

The turkeys side by side close pressed,
Watch every turn, afraid to rest,
Although there is no cause for danger,
As they must know, from the brown stranger
Who, fiercely rushing o'er the plain,
Springs high, and tumbles back again,
Or runs the huge trees sudden round,
Or tries to scale with angry bound :
Now here, now there, now up, now down,
Like any fur-clad forest clown.

And so the slow time passes on,
They, staring wild-eyed with alarm,
Although they know he cannot harm,
Grow dazed at last 'mid fear and sleep,
Their hold no longer safe can keep,
Soon stagger, fluttering to the ground,
Where Foxy crushes at a bound ;
And when the other cowards see
That they old Foxy's prey may be,
They too soon fall in traitor's maw,
The foolish victims of his paw.

Had these not been such timid folk,
They had of cunning cheats made joke.

ENVY AND LOVE.

WITHIN the shadows of a grove
Once bent a statue fair, of Love,
The modest, smiling, gentle
queen.
The doves that coo'd from tree
to tree
Were not more pure and sweet
than she,
And oft there came a flattering
crowd
That praised her charms with
raptures loud.

But close within her shadow's
ring
There lurked a snail, a noisome
thing,
Bitter with envy and with hate
That he should fill such lowly state.
Unknown, unnoticed, passed his days;
He raged to hear the statue's praise,
Longed to revenge this fancied wrong,
How find the means? the will was strong.

As midnight dimmed the moon's
faint light
Upon the figure still and white,
The snail crept near—such things
of ill
Work when the world is dark and
still.
It stole upon each limb so round,
On dimpled cheek, and hair un-
bound

Downstreaming, and with wicked care
It left a trail of blackness there.

Soon the morn rose, and in its light
All changed was yesterday's fair sight :
Each darkened feature bore a trace
That marred its purity and grace—
So swiftly envy works.   That day
Saw Beauty's friends all haste away,
And the fair statue in its place
Was left to silence and disgrace.

" Alone, alone," sad Beauty pined,
And told her troubles to the wind ;
" Why did they not this blackness prove ?
It had not borne the touch of love.
Where is the crowd that called me fair ? "
Answered the mocking breeze, " Ah, where ?
No heart was theirs, so idly they
To other charmers fled away."

'Tis ever thus that false friends fly,
Let calumny but raise its cry ;
If one true love but lingers near,
Once more the marble may be clear.

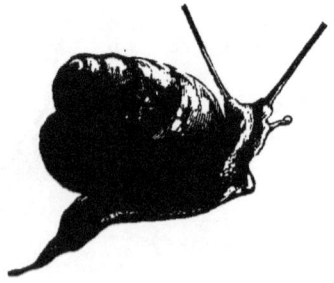

ECHO AND THE OWL.

SOLEMN owl, at midnight perched
   Within an ancient oak,
  Noticed that all around was still,
   No sound the silence broke:
   Each bird was silent in its nest,
And all the world seemed gone to rest;
Even the moon in veil of white
Hid from the world her face of light.

" Tu whit ! tu whoo !" the notes were
   oft
Repeated by the echoes round :
  The owl thought with pride,
"Nature is silent that my song
May steal its hundred groves along,
  And charm the country-side."
Then mocking echo quick replied,
" And charm, and charm the country-
   side."

Sir Owl fluttered with delight,
" Tu whit ! tu whoo !" rang through
   the night ;
  " What now, proud nightingale,
That o'er the woods have queened it
   long ;
At last you'll own my sweeter song
  To please can never fail."
Slow echo answered o'er the dale,
" To please, to please can never fail."

The lark was dreaming o'er her nest,
    While gentle Philomel, afar,
Low trilling forth her softest hymn,
    In worship of a star.
Rash owl, with unwonted fire,
Cried, " I will join the tuneful choir."
Echo was ready to repeat,
" The tuneful choir," in accents sweet.

But when the morn came, and the doves
Coo'd of their hopes, and of their loves ;
When linnet, thrush, and finches bright,
Burst in loud concert of delight ;
His " whit ! tu whoo !" poor owl raised,
Expecting to be loudly praised.
The birds, all frightened, flew away,
False echo had no word to say.

Beware an idler's praise and boast,
'Tis silent when we need it most.

WOODLAND HOMES.

THROUGH the fair pathways
   roaming,
  His heart all full of glee,
Bounded a merry schoolboy,
  From busy tasks set free.

Each woodland thing so charming,
  Its like was never seen ;
He wonder'd at the bending pines,
  The hedges, tender green.

He scrambled up so gaily
  To peep down in a nest ;
" Mama, of all the pleasant sights,
  I think I love this best.

" Ten gaping, wide mouth'd finches
  Are staring wild at me ;
How I should like to take them home,
  Their pretty ways to see!

" Suppose I used them kindly,
  And fed them on the best,
As gently as the parent birds
  That made this little nest.

"The mother would have naught
    to do
  But rest and sing all day,
And when the ten are older grown,
  They all might fly away."

With eager hands uplifted,
  The boy glanced down on me,
His bright young face set beaming
  By the treasure in the tree.

"Child, pause while I remind you
  Of what you undertake ;
Maybe you'll let the nest remain,
  For yours and birdies' sake.

"You mean to act most kindly
  To these poor noisy elves,
That with weak, unfledged pinions,
  May no way help themselves.

"Can you wake with the dawning,
  And set the nest to right ?
Then start to find the thousand
    things
  They'll want twixt morn and
    night ?

"Remember, though but little
  They need, yet oft that need ;
Strange insects, all deep hidden
  In core, and root, and weed.

"Then can you share quite fairly,
  'Twixt ten chicks out of breath,
That some may not be fed too
    much,
  While others starve to death?

"If you would fill a mother's
    part—
  A bird does this with joy,
It is not reckoned toil by her,
  She loves such work, my boy.

"At length, when falling shadows
  May threaten midnight storm,
Can you spread out protecting
    wings,
  To keep them safe and warm ?

"And can you trill the lullaby,
  The baby-birds' good night ?
If you can do all this, and more,
  Then take the nest, 'tis right."

My son, with empty fingers,
  Came smiling down to me ;
"Mama, you're right, a birdie's
    work
  Is not a child's, I see."

THE OAK; OR, PRIDE AND HUMILITY.

A MIDNIGHT storm raged through the wood,
　　Like wild beast in its lair,
One in its fiercest, maddest mood,
　　Of sullen rash despair;
All bent before its power and might,
　　Except the forest king—
The oak, in pride, stood all upright
　　To face this faceless thing.
It tore the oak-tree from its hold,
　　Then flung it in the stream,
And left it there, a trophy bold,
　　Fading at morning's beam;
The morn that rose so calm and bright,
To show the reeds this cruel sight,
The trembling reeds, that whispering said,
" Here lies King Oak, dethroned and dead."

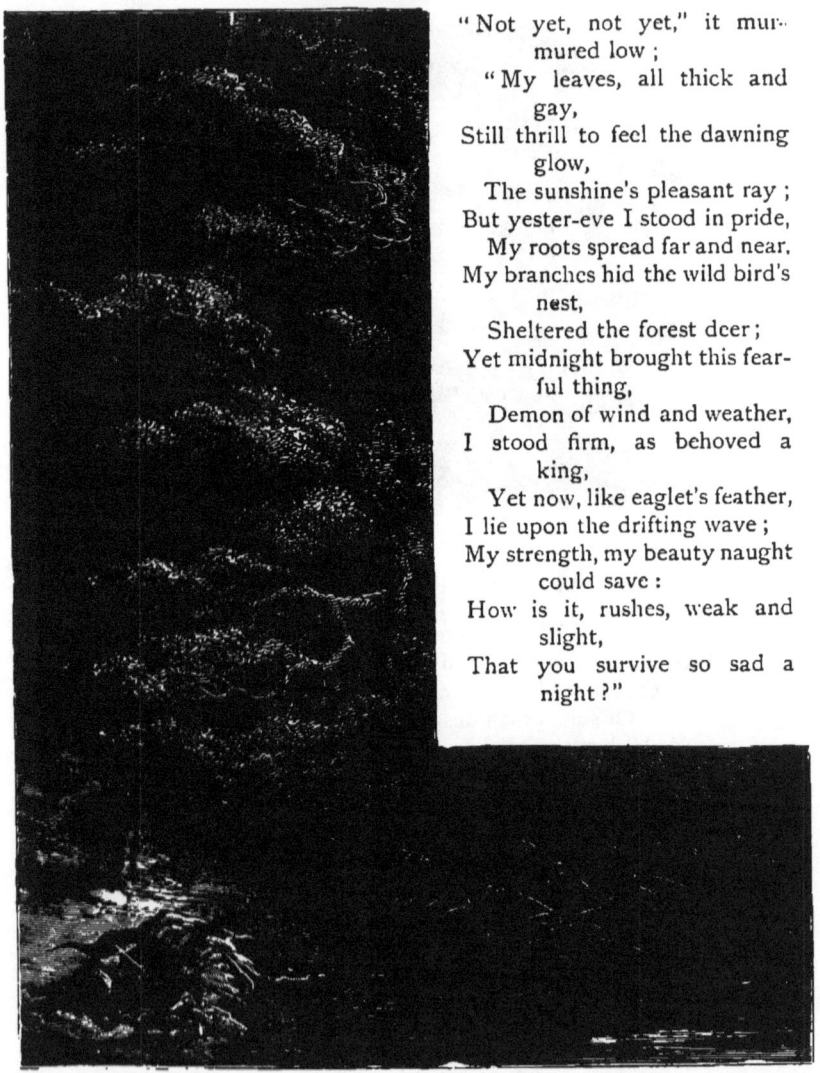

"Not yet, not yet," it mur-
mured low ;
"My leaves, all thick and
gay,
Still thrill to feel the dawning
glow,
The sunshine's pleasant ray ;
But yester-eve I stood in pride,
My roots spread far and near.
My branches hid the wild bird's
nest,
Sheltered the forest deer ;
Yet midnight brought this fear-
ful thing,
Demon of wind and weather,
I stood firm, as behoved a
king,
Yet now, like eaglet's feather,
I lie upon the drifting wave ;
My strength, my beauty naught
could save :
How is it, rushes, weak and
slight,
That you survive so sad a
night ?"

The voice grew faint, the leaves unmoved,
　The pitying reeds bent near,
Pale lilies breathed their sweet perfume,
　The fallen king to cheer;
And as the sorrowing breezes stole
　Softly o'er dale and hill,
They gently kissed each broken branch
　That lay there, crushed and still.
"Ye answer not, ye answer not:
　Why was it that I fell?—
I was so strong to hold my own—
　Tell me, and then farewell."
The bending rushes sadly spoke,
"Our secret was but simple, oak—
We humbly bowed before the blast;
You braved it, to lie low at last."

THE LITTLE YELLOW FINCH.

A BIRD-CATCHER has trained a thrush
    Its fellows to decoy
        By song,
And many come with headlong rush,
    Caught, prisoned by the boy
        Ere long.

His traps are light, while spread around
    And freely scattered
        Are seeds,
Which lie there on the ground ;
    No scarecrow tattered
        Misleads.

Too soon they all are caught but one,
    A little yellow finch
        So sweet,
That clings quite near, as though in fun,
    The traps within an inch,
        " Tweet ! tweet !"

"Do peck some food, 'tis all prepared,"
  Tempts decoy, half in rage,
      Half tired,
Knowing that till this bird is snared
  He starves in hidden cage
      Close wired.

"Rich seeds heaped up, come, dear, peck;"
  But Goldie cries, low
      Mocking,
"What, try to trap poor friends—to wreck
  Their lives like yours—oh,
      Shocking!

"Yon tempting bait is spread in vain,
  I know there is a snare
      Hid near;
When men, without a reason plain,
  Make us their care,
      I fear.

"Whene'er I see too great a gain
  Offered for naught
      I sigh,
Knowing it means but loss and pain
  And trusting birdies caught.
      Good-bye,
          Poor treacherous thrush,
      Good-bye!"

"WHO SEEKS SHALL FIND."

AN old man, worn, and grey, and very bent
    With storm of years,
Called to his side his mourning sons,
    And, 'mid their tears,
Bade them farewell : " My light is set,
Yours has not risen yet.

"The fair estate my fathers left to me,
    I give it you ;
But charge ye, sell or share it not,
    Or all will rue ;
For somewhere, hidden deep within the ground,
A treasure may be found.

" Gold, honest gold, my sons : it lies not far—
    I know it, mind ;
Plough, till, and turn the earth early or late—
    ' Who seeks shall find :'

Be not dismayed, though it take time and care—
I tell you, boys, 'tis there."

E'en as he spoke he gently passed away,
    In peace with all ;
And spring-tide came before those three tall sons
    His words recall :
Then all united vowed to find the gold
Of which their father told.

Early and late the brothers toiled together
    With willing hand,
The ground upturning oft and well,
    That hopeful band ;
Still seeking, though it seemed but search all vain,
In sunshine or in rain.

An old man's wisdom is the truest lore
    For youth to trust ;
So these three proved, as year by year they sought,
    Toiling on, just
As they at first had done : no coins they found,
Yet nodding sheaves grew round.

They raised such harvests that the country folk
    Looked on amazed,
For none had deemed rare wheat as this
    Could here be raised ;
So tall and fine, it glowed like the bright gold
For which at length 'twas sold.

Once, as they counted o'er their piled-up gains,
    In winter's leisure,
Spoke one, " I wonder if these welcome crowns
    Are father's treasure
We've dug and ploughed for long ? it's in my mind
He said, ' Who seeks shall find.' "

" Yes," cried his brothers, " now the riddle's read :
    He was not wrong;
These coins were hid, indeed, deep in the earth
    We searchèd long,
Unwitting that the toil we thought so vain
Was raising golden grain."

HAND AND HEART.

TWO little swallows built a nest—
 So neat behind, before—
In thatch and straw that shaded well
 A rustic cottage door.
They built it firm, they built it strong,
 With feathers, grass, and clay,
And soon five mottled eggs were laid
 Upon a happy day.

And soon five downy heads were seen,
 Soon five beaks open'd wide ;
You should have watched that fluttering pair,
 Their happiness and pride.
But sudden came a cruel hand
 That stole the chicks away,
Changing the sunshine into gloom,
 One mournful, wretched day.

Oh, heedless hand, that brought such woe
 Into a birdie's nest !
Oh, thoughtless heart, that caused such grief
 In helpless feathered breast !
What gain was yours ?—five twitt'ring things,
 Too soon to droop and die,
That now had filled their home with song,
 Had you but passed them by.

JUSTICE.

WO tabbies on a summer morn
    Were gaily walking,
When, lo, a boy let fall a cheese
    While busy talking :
Both wandered near, as though in play,
And slyly rolled that cheese away.

They rolled it fast, they rolled it far,
    Those cunning cats ;
They rolled it to the forest's edge,
    By dint of pats ;
But when they came to share, you see,
These foolish Toms could not agree.

Each one, mistrusting much the other,
    Began to growl,
And made so loud a din and noise,
    They woke an owl :
He cried, " Don't fight, but let us tell
Your case to Lawyer Judge-'em-well."

So said, so done ; a monkey came
    When they did call,
With ink and pen, and scales in hand,
    To settle all
"Are you the folks who disagree,
Give here the cheese, and trust to me."

He broke the mass, dropped either half
    In balance flat.
One lowest plumped, " Now, see how law
    Will alter that."
He bit a huge piece off, and plain
They saw him weigh the rest again.

" Now this side's wrong ; " another nibble
      Made that too light.
" Stop ! " cried the cats ; " why, at the rate
      At which you bite,
We soon shall have no cheese to share :
Surely that is not dealing fair."

" Justice must have its dues," cried he,
      Still biting ;
" You should have shared your cheese in peace,
      Instead of fighting :
The two sides I have matched, and for my fee
All that is left belongs to me."

THE DREAM TREASURE.

WHANG, the dingy, stingy old
    miller,
So dearly he loved money,
He ſain would have gathered it all
    the day,
    As a wild bee does its honey;
But, unlike the bee that from garden
    and wood
Collects all its sweets for the general
    good,
Whang would have garnered his much-
    prized pelf
For the sole delight of his miserly self.
    No music for him had the merry din
    Of the wheel, as it turned his bread
      to win.

As Whang the miller sat at the door
    Of the wheesy and creaky mill,
Which had stood so long by the murmuring stream
    That was seldom or never still,
He sighed and he grumbled, "The times are bad—
Worse, I am sure, than when *I* was a lad,
For then I seemed to have money to spend,
But now I would much rather borrow than lend,
    For though the mill-wheel goes round and round,
    It brings but a penny where I want a pound."

"Whang," cried a neighbour, hurrying past,
" Kind ſortune is my friend at last:
Three times have I dreamt that a bucket oſ gold
Hid 'neath our hearthstone, cracked and old.
Twice have I scorned the warning plain,
But yet last night it came again.

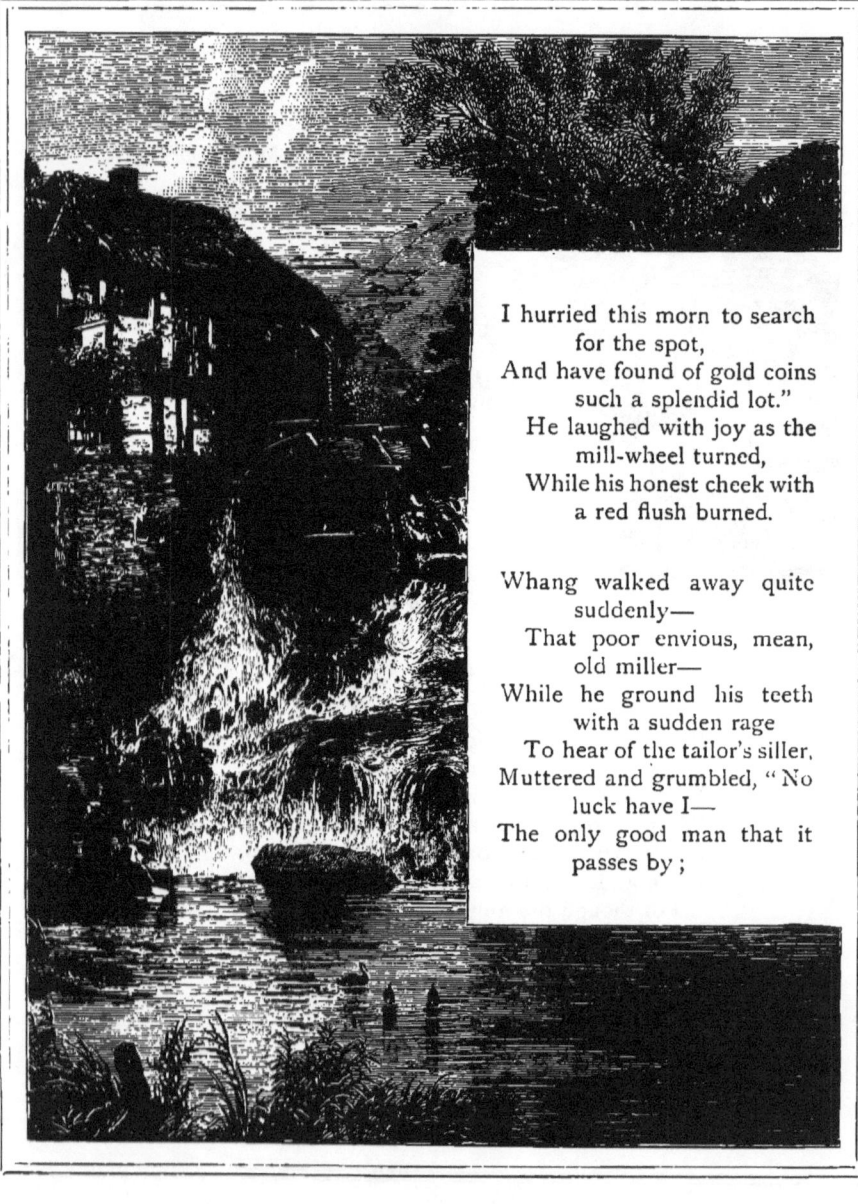

I hurried this morn to search
for the spot,
And have found of gold coins
such a splendid lot."
He laughed with joy as the
mill-wheel turned,
While his honest cheek with
a red flush burned.

Whang walked away quite
suddenly—
That poor envious, mean,
old miller—
While he ground his teeth
with a sudden rage
To hear of the tailor's siller,
Muttered and grumbled, "No
luck have I—
The only good man that it
passes by;

Though if I of treasure could three times dream,
It might bring me more coins than yon noisy stream,
  That falls with a whirr and a constant dash :
  I had much rather hear the chink of hard cash."

Then Whang, the miserly, foolish miller,
  Wasted many a precious hour—
He no longer went tending his mill aright,
  Or grinding his customers' flour—
But lolled with his pipe by doorpost or beam,
Longing for night, that perchance he might
    dream—
For he truly believed that a vision thrice-told
Could betoken naught else but deep-buried
    gold ;
  And though the mill-wheel turned busily
    round,
The miller no longer noticed its sound.

Now every hour that Whang could keep
In bed, he did, and tried to sleep ;
Oft glittering visions becrowded his brain,
Rested there, and soon fled again ;
His workmen grew idle, his customers cross,
His profits were surely all turning to loss ;
Yet ever he thought, " I a treasure shall find,
When the selfsame dream three times comes to my mind,
  And then I will bid farewell to the mill,
  And yonder old wheel may turn round at its will."

To Whang at last the bright vision came—
  A chest of gold.   He saw it hid
Deep under his mill ; would the dream come again ?
  Yes, that very same night it did :
Now who would mock at and call him absurd ?
Would it come once again ? Yes, it came on the third.

He rose all a-tremble, took lantern and spade,
Stole down to the cellar, his plans ready laid.
  No sound was heard but the drip and fall
  Of waters that splashed near the old mill-wall.

He would keep his secret, and hide the gold,
  Nor aught of his fortune tell ;
He would heap it and keep it all his own,
  The red gold he loved so well.
He dug in the darkness, unheeded, alone ;
He dug till he came to a blackened stone ;
For many and many a tedious hour,
He tossed the mould in a musty shower.
  Silenced now was the noisy clatter
  Of the busy drops falling all a-scatter.

Whang, in his cellar so dark and deep,
  Toiled until ready to drop ;
Whenever he thought of his new-found gold,
  Poor miser, he could not stop.
He dug and he dug at that ancient stone,
Though often he stopped to grumble and groan,
When a beam crossed here and a beam held there—
This treasure must surely be rich and rare.
  No noise he heard, not even the sound
  Of the creaking mill-wheel turning slowly round.

Whang, through the long and the weary hours,
  Dug deep till the morning light
Stole in, and showed that bar, rivet, and stone
  Had stirred—'twas a welcome sight.
His fingers trembled ; one effort—'tis past,
The huge stone was stirred from its place at last :
His treasure, his treasure, now, now he should see—
He hauled the mass from its hidden bonds free.

Then a crash, a smash, and a sudden fall,
  The crazy mill toppled over ;

It fell down a heap all of timber and dust,
   Crushing the daisies and clover ;
It fell with a din and a mighty smother,
That woke all the neighbours, who cried to each other,
" 'Tis the end of the world, now, whate'er shall we do ?"
Then breathlessly waited, for nobody knew.

Not the end of the world, of course not that,
   But the end of that poor old mill,
For Whang its foundations had dug at so well,
   He had stirred them at length by his skill ;
The home, though despised, that had brought him his bread,
He had helped to destroy.   Soon, with badly bruised head,
They found him yet groping, 'mid timber and beam,
Seeking still for the treasure that was but a dream.

TRUE JUSTICE.

THE mighty Caliph Al Mahoun
  In proud Bagdad kept court ;
And there he built a palace fair,
A marble palace rich and rare,
    By cunning workmen wrought.
Gold, jasper, azure, ruby gleams
    Adorned the floor and wall,
While scented fountains poured
    their streams
    'Mid stately columns tall :
From far and near came crowds
    to see
How grand a palace home might
    be.

'Tis whispered that the glorious sun
  Has spots upon its face :
The palace of great Al Mahoun,
  Although so rare a place,
Had one sad blemish—at its door
There dwelt a weaver, old and poor,
In a mud hut his sires had raised.
The royal wall it almost grazed,
Yet though the caliph's servants sought
To buy it, it could not be bought.

" Slaves, give him what there is to give,
  And sweep the den away ;
A traitor, to oppose his lord,
Fearless of bowstring and of cord ;
If he object, the headsman show,
That he more tractable may grow !"
So cried the vizier in a rage,
Till stopped by Al Mahoun the sage.
" Ourselves will hear this weaver's tale—
Justice in Bagdad should prevail."

The poor man came; a purse of gold
Was offered for his mansion old,
But still he shook his turbaned head,
" I cannot sell it, sirs," he said ;
" Here in this hut my sires were
    born,
Here passed my manhood's happy
    morn,
Here mother, brother, children, wife
Have lived and died, and this pooɪ
    life
My lord may take, ere I resign
The home that ever has been mine."

He spoke, and knelt upon the
    ground,
While silent bent the courtiers
    round.
" But, weaver, with this treasure
    great
Go buy yourself a proud estate."

"I need no treasure, rich my lot
While I can toil in yon poor cot.
Sultan, my head, I know, is thine
To take or leave: the hut is mine,
Dearer to me than aught on earth;
Without it life were little worth."

The guards drew near, all in that room
Waited to hear the words of doom;
But Al Mahoun—on whom be grace!—
Turned to the man a patient face,
And, stretching forth his royal hand,
Signalled the suppliant to stand.
"Weaver, 'tis well; thy home to me
Is sacred as a mosque could be—
I would not touch one stick or stone,
Thou speakest truth, they are thine own.

"Thine, as is mine the palace proud,
Where each day press a loyal crowd;
Thine, and, though at that palace door,
Many may think it blot and sore,
It shall remain for ever thine,
Though fain I would the cot were mine,
That gold could buy or words persuade,
But threat or bowstring shall not aid.
Depart, good weaver—never fear,
Justice to Al Mahoun is dear;—

"For when a stranger's wondering gaze
Surveys my palace with amaze,
And asks what rich and mighty king
Has planned this fair and wondrous thing,
Has raised the marble column tall,
Or fountains, where sweet waters fall,
Though some around may scornful prate,
And sneer at Al Mahoun the Great,
When their eyes meet this hut they must
To the brave name of Great add 'Just,'"

GOD'S TOKENS.

A LITTLE bunch of snowdrops
     Murmured, "Sweet,
What can we do but wither at thy
     feet?
The dainty rose may please, the
     myrtle crown,
     But we, low down,
Must all unheeded bloom, by
     faded bowers
Still useless lie, the wan spring's
     palest flowers;
     No pleasant fate is ours!"

"Be still, ye trembling snowdrops!
     He who made you
Gave you a holy errand upon earth—
Sent you to tell His weary mortal children,
     All faint-hearted,
Of the New Year's sweet, ne'er-failing birth;
To teach that all things by His hand may grow
     That brought you through the snow,—

"So weak, and white, and fearful,
     Humbly bending
Patient before each shower and icy blast,
Bending, yet ever rising in fresh beauty
     When storms are past—
A pure and simple type of that great wonder,
True faith, that lies deep in the Christian's heart,
     With life ne'er to depart!"

THE PEACOCK'S TAIL.

Sir Eagle, kite, and vulture
    Took the foremost place;
Magpie, jay, and blackbird,
    Owl, with solemn face,

Fluttered; wren and robin,
    Thrush and skylark, too;
Finch, jackdaw, and starling,
    Jay, and brown cuckoo;

ALL the birds assembled,
    Came from far and near;
Something quite important
    Troubled them, 'twas clear.

While a thousand others
    Made the forest ring:
All this great assembly
    Met to choose a king!

There was much contention,
  And they differed long—
Some were for fine feathers,
  Some for sweetest song—

Till the peacock's plumage
  Caught their foolish eyes,
Causing all, with one accord,
  To give that bird the prize.

They hail'd him with acclaim,
  Approv'd with clapping wing:
The tiniest voted loud,
  "The Peacock for our king!"

But Jackdaw, that aspired
  Lord Chancellor to be,
Said, questions he must ask
  Before he could agree.

"Fair sir, and almost sire,
  Tell us, what would you do,
Should danger threaten Birdland,
  While all depends on you?

"Rebellions might arise,
  Or perils yet unknown,
When all must turn for strength
  To him who fills the throne.

"Sir, in the people's name,
  I venture here to say,
How would you dare or do
  If foe-birds came our way?"

The noisy cheers were hushed
  As Jackdaw wisely spoke;
Scarcely half a twitter
  The sudden silence broke.

The Peacock stared about,
  His thoughts seemed all to fail.
"If I were king, I would—
  I would spread out my tail!"

"And then?"   "Oh, then, of
    course—
  Sir Jackdaw, do not rail!—

If danger threatened Birdland
  I'd fold my handsome tail!"

A sudden hiss arose,
  All jeered the silly bird;
They found to name him king
  Would be a thing absurd.

All beauty is but vain
  Nor sense nor heart being near:
A Peacock may be fine,
  But foolish too, I fear.

THE GREAT AND LITTLE KINGS.

ANOTHER meeting soon was
    named,
  Merit should now decide;
So all the birdies, as before,
  Came pressing, side by side.

They twittered long, they twittered
    loud,
  But could not yet agree,
Till up spoke Jackdaw once again—
  A clever bird was he.

"Let us not differ, friends," he said,
  "But to decide all try;
And choose for king the bird that flies
  The nearest to the sky."

"Hear, hear! We will," the answer came
  From many a feathered thing;
"The one that to the sun can rise,
  That one shall be our king."

Up, up, there flew a dizzy crowd,
  That soon began to thin;
The Lark and Eagle still uprose,
  One of them safe to win.

The Eagle's wings are large and strong,
  His eyes can meet the sun;
Soon Lark gave up, the birds all cried,
  "Hurrah! The Eagle's won!

Up, up, he still ascends, 'tis clear,"
  And loud the cheers arise;
"Hail to King Eagle!" filled the air,
  "The monarch of the skies."

Then cried a Wren, "No; *I* am king!"
  The birds all chirped with glee,
For it, perched on the Eagle's head,
  Had flown as high as he!

"Nay, higher," piped the saucy Wren,
  Giving a little spring;

"I'm far above the Eagle here:
  Surely you'll crown me king?"

The Eagle mocked, "Then, king, descend
  To earth without my aid."
"Oh, no!" chirped Wren; "indeed, good
    bird,
  I dare not—I'm afraid.

"Pray, only land me safe again,
  The crown is yours, not mine;
You won it by a bold, brave flight,
  I but by cunning fine."

And since that day the Eagle rules ;
While Wren, the tiny thing,
Is known to all as " Regulus,"
Which means the " Little King."

THE BOASTER.

ROCKET flew up mid the stars,
Past Saturn and Mars,
" See," it cried, "what a fine track of light
Marks my path, all so dazzling and bright !
Now, stars, who will notice your spark
When MY radiance glows mid the dark ?
Or if some *do* notice, 'tis only to mock it,
For what is a star to a beautiful rocket ? "

Repeating its bold noisy say
Mid the cloudlets grey,
Proudly the visitor fluttered,
Till Orion angrily muttered,
And Dog-Star took up the dispute,
And mocked at the stranger, that, mute
And confused, burned quite dimly with fear,
While the planets all merrily twinkled to hear.

" A ' rocket bold !' a thing of earth
And of little worth,
That is flung among us, a sudden light,
To fall and flutter and die in the night ;
Boaster, be still, never journey so far
To compare thyself to a shining star,
For although thine ascent to the heavens be quick,
Just as sudden thy fall, a poor blackened stick."

NATURE'S MIRACLE.

"MIRACLE! a miracle!
   I would that I might see—
I marvel if so strange a thing
   Still wrought on earth could be."

So mused a caliph, as he strolled
   In palace garden fair,
Where shadows of the palm-trees tall
   Fell cool on lilies rare,

Where marble columns stately rose,
   Where fountains trickled slow,
While the sweet landscape seemed afire
   Beneath the sunset's glow.

E'en as he mused an aged form
   Came slowly by his way—
The famed As-roud, who read the stars,
   And told of peace or fray.

"A miracle! a miracle!
   Come, old man bent and wise,
That rumour hath magician named,
   Bring one before mine eyes.

"My slaves shall give thee great reward
    Of gem or golden crown;
But shouldst thou fail—the river's deep,
    And false pretenders drown."

"Light of the East," the old man cried,
    In accents grave and low,
"I care not for thy promised gold,
    Thy river's silent flow.

"A miracle! a miracle!
    Proud master of all Ind,
I'll show thee one without reward,
    The greatest of its kind.

"Rest thou within this arbour fair,
    Which breezes softly fan,
And thou shalt see a mighty work
    Could ne'er be wrought by man.

"Lay thy veiled head upon thine hand,
    While I a circle draw,
And summon here, my spells to aid,
    A power heeds not thy law."

The caliph's eyes grew dim, as traced
The magic circle round;
Then, lo, he saw a wondrous thing
Take place upon the ground.

First rose a shoot, a tiny spray,
Then, swift as eye could see,
The slender thing shot up aloft,
A tall, luxuriant tree.

And ere the wondering glance could rest
Upon its branches fair,
The tree was hung with golden fruit,
All tempting, ripe, and rare.

The caliph stretched his hand to touch,
When, lo, on every side,
A thousand trees had sprung from one,
In orchards spreading wide.

Upon the rosy, blushing fruit
The caliph gazed with awe,
Then, turning in his wonderment,
The strange old man he saw.

"A miracle! a miracle!
Hath passed before mine eyes!
Thy power hath fulfilled my wish,
Thine be reward and prize."

"O mighty monarch of the East,
A miracle, 'tis true;
Thy dial's face will give the time
It takes such work to do."

The caliph looked, a rusty thing
Lay tarnished in his hand;
The saplings into trees had grown,
And changed seemed all the land.

The arbour where he late reclined
Seemed moss-grown now, and worn;
His very garments, royal robes,
Looked weather-stained and torn.

He rose with trembling lip and limb;
"What's this? what's this?" he cried.
"It is the miracle time works,"
Said As-roud, by his side.

"Sire, is it less a miracle,
Though forty years be past,
That a small seed dropped in the earth
Should bloom a tree at last,

"All decked with glowing, rosy fruit
To tempt both lips and eye,
Then thousandfold itself repeat,
Against the summer sky?

"Great Nature's miracles, each day
In silent order found,
In earth, in air, in watery deep,
Through Nature's magic round.

"You crave for wonders, they are
      near:
   List to the wild bird's song,
The rippling river that reflects
    Each cloud that glides along.

'Watch these, Omar, and as you
      watch
   Think of the mighty Hand
That rules them all, but seek no
      more
   Its workings to command.

"My lord awake;" he raised his
      wand,
   The youthful monarch stood
Where rose the marble column
      tall,
   Where frowned the cypress
      wood.

Fair lilies in the sunset waved,
   The fountains trickled still;
Scarce had the sun-dial's shadow
      changed
   Since Omar had his will.

THE WISE MOTHER-BIRD.

"MAMA, the farmer came to-day,
    And seemed so busy talking,
The while his wife and little sons
    Quite near our nest were walking;
He said he would his neighbours call
To come and help him, one and all.
What shall we do? where shall we run,
When once the harvest has begun?"

So chirped four tiny callow larks,
    In hasty, trembling fear.
"My pretty ones, be calm, there's time,
    No pressing danger's near;

You'll stronger grow ere neighbours' hand
To level this fine bearded land
Finds leisure—darlings, do not cry,
There is no need when mother's nigh."

" Mama, the farmer came again,"
   They twittered, anxious all;
Pressing to meet her as she dropped
   From Heaven, like feathered ball ;
" He looked across the field of gold,
And said he had his kinfolk told
To bring machines—those frightful things—
When they had time—yet weak our wings.

Piped Madam Lark, with easy tone,
   "Cheer up, sweet chicks, all's well ;
Yet, listen, dears, when I'm away,
   And mind each word you tell:

There is no need to fret and flurry,
Neighbours, kinsmen, seldom hurry,
And you may yet have time to grow,
Ere friends and engines come to mow."

"Mama, the farmer just has past,
   Declaring that to-morrow
The work begins, for off at once
   He'd go, and wagons borrow
To cart away the corn and barley."
"Enough, 'twill take him time to parley;
The horses will be all in use,
And wagon-owners make excuse."

"Mama, the farmer, scythe in hand,
   Has summoned his own men,
And vowed to-morrow with the dawn
   He'd come himself, and then,
That ere the eve his golden grain
Must lie in heaps upon the plain,
For all should work with main and might."
Said Mother Lark, "Prepare for flight.

"Now we must leave this snug retreat,
   For strong has grown each feather;
Come, follow me, my darlings, quick—
   We'll hide amid the heather:
While farmer spoke, in tones elate,
Of friends and neighbours, we could wait,

But when he takes the scythe in hand,
Not long the nodding grain will stand."

Soon with a twitter and loud bustle,
　　Their pretty nest they leave ;
The four delighted with the change,
　　Old Lark inclined to grieve.
" Dear little home, I o'er you hung,
As up at heaven's high gate I sung,
Raising my voice in thankful glee,
For all you held so dear to me.

" Dear little home, with poppies crowned,
　　Where my sweet young ones lay,
I'm sad to leave, yet for their sake
　　I hasten far away.
My fledglings four, come quick, I see
The twilight spreading o'er the lea ;
When the dawn rises pink and clear
The cruel sickle may be here."

" Why, mother," asked the birdies four,
　　When they drew close that night,
And lay beneath her soft brown wings,
　　Still panting with their flight—
" Why were you in such sudden haste
To lead us to this purple waste ?
Each hour we felt us growing stronger ;
Why not have stayed a little longer ?—

" Why, why ?" they chirped, each nodding head
　　Close nestling to her side ;
" 'Tis two good weeks since first he came,
　　Why not two more abide ?—
Why, why ?" "My chicks, in safety rest—
Mothers know ' why ' and what is best ;
' Why ' has but one good answer—' must ;'
'Tis ours to *do*, 'tis yours to trust."

THE DISGUISED WOLF.

ONCE, a tired shepherd slept
    In a deep, cosy nook;
By there came a crafty wolf,
    Stole his coat and crook;
Took his hat and pan-pipes too—
'T was a clever scheme, and new!

"But the shepherd might awake"
    Urged the wolf's sly wit;
"I must lure the flock afar:
    Question, way most fit?"
Sheep are foolish, meek, and
    mild—
Creatures easily beguiled.

Oft the shepherd sweetly sang—
    Well this Sir Lupus knew—
Gentle ditties as he led
    His soft, woolly crew.
"I will sing, and they will follow,
Be it over hill or hollow.

"Then, before the shepherd rouses,
    Soon will I eat my fill,
For the tender little lambies
    I will quickly kill;
My dark den, deep in the wood,
I will store with mutton good."

Lupus caught the fallen pipes,
  Raised his voice in song ;
But, alas ! that voice was wolf-like,
  Telling what was wrong :
Up the sleeping shepherd bounded,
Soon the traitor's howls resounded.

Fast tangled in the jacket,
  Smothered in the hat,
Lupus could not run as usual—
  Down the blows came, pat !

Dressed up as an honest man,
Awkwardly the creature ran.

" I'll teach you," cried the shep-
      herd,
  " To show such thievish skill
In your own guise, for wolf will
      out,
  Conceal it how you will !
Those that do wicked things must
      take
Their punishment or soon or late."

HOW HE MIGHT BE IMPROVED.

"I THINK," said a nag, as a
    ramble he took,
That brought him one day
    to the edge of a brook—
" I think that a horse is a beautiful
    sight,
With its long flowing mane, and its
    steps bounding light ;
Yet still, if *I* formed one in beauty
    to rove,
I could slightly improve on the
    work of Great Jove :—

Its legs should be longer, the better to race ;
More slender perhaps, and possessed of more grace ;
Then its neck, too, the surer more nobly to rear,
Should curved, like the neck of a tall swan, appear ;
Its strong chest should broaden, to show all the might
That a horse would possess, were he only formed right.
That is all I would alter," he added ; " yet no ;
For as on its back men a-riding must go,
Why not grow a saddle, or something as good,
More easy to carry than leather or wood ?
These are some of the changes that fain I would see
Great Jupiter make."   Cried a voice, " Let them be.
But wait till you all these improvements behold,
On the steed that your master has fashioned of old."
A great whirl of dust came, and from it arose
A creature the oddest of any that grows ;
So tall, strange, and awkward, the horse shrank away,
And trembled to see it, a monster in grey.
He shook at the creature Jove fashioned, to show
How foolish are those who presume all to know,
And would fain teach their maker his work is not true,
As though greater wonders themselves they could do.
" Here is your fancied charger, its legs longer grown ;
Much thinner, yet hardly more graceful, you'll own ;

Its neck, too, is altered ; far broader its chest—
Just as you wished, arching, yet scarce for the best.
See, a fine living saddle, that never needs change,
Although man from morning to even should range.
Now, give but one nod, I can change you to this."
The listener trembled, as by an abyss.
" Have mercy, Great Jove, spare my race and spare me!
Oh, never again will I dictate to thee ;
Thy works must be perfect, for thou best canst tell
What form and what features thy creatures suit well."
" Go, then ; I forgive, for thy true shame I see.
Creatures once formed, formed for ever must be ;
And as to thy whim this owes hump and ill form,
That dooms him to wander o'er Egypt's hot storm,
His race for the future shall terrify thine,
His strength shall surpass that of horses so fine,
While true men will tell of the rash steed that strove
To improve on the creature designed by Great Jove."

THE MOUSE TRANSFORMED.

THIS little mouse to Mirza came—
   A great enchanter he :
" Sir, I am told you can transform
   Creatures small like me.
A mouse leads but a troubled life,
For pussies cause him woe and strife :
Change me, sir, into a cat."
'Twas done ; a tabby, mousie sat.

But soon the cat no pleasure found,
   Lest a dog should worry,
So half her time she spent in fear,
   Half in watchful flurry.
Mirza saw her pining round :
" Puss," he said, " unto a hound
I will change you, safe and sound,
Then for fear you'll have no ground."

The dog, of strong and handsome
    kind,
  Enjoyed himself an hour,
But then he heard some hunters
    boast
Of tiger's strength and power—
How it could men and dogs de-
    stroy.
Gone was poor Carlo's peace and
    joy:
" A tiger may upon me rush,
And every bone within me crush."
Off to Mirza he did jog,
" Oh, let me not remain a dog!"

"How, nervous still, what would
    you crave ? "
  " A tiger, Mirza, let me
    be."
A royal tiger soon he stood,
  In shadow of the thicket
    free ;
All forest creatures fled before,
And trembled at his echoing
    roar :
Grown strong, he ravaged at
    his will,
Poor helpless things to tear
    and kill,
Till huntsmen gathered on his
    track,
And swore the creature to
    attack.

Once more to Mirza's side he
    crept,
  And sighed, with abject head,

" I cannot, dare not, face the foe—.
    Their weapons sharp I dread ;
Change me to something else, I pray,
That I may safely hide away :
Mighty magician, thou art great,
Save me, oh, save me from this fate ;
I feel the self-same terror that
I felt ere changed into a cat."

" For shame, thou weak and abject thing- -
    No change was wrought in thee ;
I gave thee form of tiger king,
    It may not hide, I see,
The self-same timorous coward heart
That best befits a mouse's part ;
Thou art but brave o'er meaner things,
For cruelty to meanness clings ;
No power can make thee true and bold :
Once more a mouse be, as of old."

THE OBSTINATE PAIR.

TWO goats upon a morning
  Went off to spend a day,
But, as it happ'd, a slender bridge
  Lay stretched across the way :
It spanned a torrent, deep and wide,
And one goat came on either side.

" *I* shan't go back," cried Softy White ;
  " I'm quite as good as you."
" May be," said Patch, " but I shall cross
  This bridge, that's certain—true."
So each stepped on, until half way
They met, upon the fir-tree grey.

There was not room, squeeze how they would,
  To pass on side by side,
So each began to push and butt,
  All heedless, in their pride,

That underneath the fallen tree
A torrent foamed all wild and free.

They struggled long as best they could,
   Cried Softy, "You go back."
" I won't," said Patch ; " pray, who are you,
   That I should clear your track ? "
They pushed and twisted with long horn,
   Then tried with jump and skip,
Each would be first, so in the end
   They both did over slip.

They slipped and fell, their foolish pride
   Had cost them each a life ;
The waters bore them both away,
   Cold victims to their strife.

THE PARROT AND THE DOVE.

FAMOUS Eastern king had one sweet child,
      A darling boy ;
His parrot, too, had a beloved one,
      Her feathered joy ;
And all day long the youthful prince would play
      With this live talking toy :
Both were such friends, they could not live asunder ;
Their fond affection was the whole court's wonder.

Till some one gave the child another pet,
      A foreign dove,
With bending neck, and softly cooing notes—
      A pretty gentle love ;
Young parrot was neglected, cast aside,
      Like an old worn-out glove :
He fretted, scolded at his rival fair,
She to torment him made it all her care.

For dove that was so pretty, was but foolish
      In parrot's eyes ;

She flaunted his disgrace, " I'm best liked now,"
     A speech unkind, unwise :
" Every one says you're but a common thing,
While I'm admired by courtier, prince, and king."

One day the quarrel grew to such a pitch,
     That in a rage
The parrot clutched the dove, and left her strangled
     Low in her golden cage.
Bad deeds on bad deeds follow, for the boy
     Came running at this stage.
Finding the dove dead, in his passion wild
He seized her foe, and killed old Polly's child.

The parent bird—ah, how poor parents grieve
     When wrong is done
By children's fault !—at once flew to relieve
     Her hapless son ;
Forgot all else, and sought to have revenge
     Upon this cruel one :
The darling, once so favoured, him to save,
At the boy's eyes two fatal pecks she gave.

Ah me ! but passion is a fearful master
     Of bird or king !
Loud through the palace, at this sad disaster,
     Sudden sad cries did ring.
Old Polly, sick with grief, flew far away,
     With heavy heart and wing ;
While father, servants, hurried to the room.
The scene that met them filled their minds with gloom.

I cannot paint it, or the wild despair
     Of bitter might
That filled the monarch's heart, to see his son
     In such a dreadful plight.
" Where is the wretched traitor hath done this,
     Our royal hopes to blight ?

Old Polly say you ? Kill her !" "Nay! but, sire,
She's perched on pine-tree safe, none can get nigh her."

Some weeks went by, and still the poor bird hid
      On tree-top tall ;
No honeyed words, or bait of favourite food,
      Or over-friendly call,
Could e'er entice her—did she guess the king
      Five golden crowns in all
Had promised for her capture ? I can't say ;
But she eluded them from day to day.

His majesty grew angry : " Not killed yet !
      'Tis most absurd !
Of all my idle train, can no one capture
      This foolish spiteful bird ?

I'll go myself."   Hiding his sword, he went,
  On slaying Poll intent ;
Yet calling, as he came the pine-trees near,
" My dear old friend, my pretty Poll, come here."

" No, sire," said Poll, whose deep voice sounded hoarsely
  Far o'er the crowd ;
" I know too well there's bitter feud between us—
  Your kindness is too loud.
Our children each at fault, yet mine was helpless,
  And yours so strong and proud.
To save my own, evil to yours I wrought :
No mortal can repay such wrong with gentle thought."

" Parrot, I'll all forget, and all forgive,
  If you'll come here ;
I'll show you something that will instant prove
  You have no cause for fear."
" I spy that ' something,' tis a hidden sword—
  'Twould prove the case too clear ;
Sorrow and trouble have we caused each other—
You can revenge, but I my grief must smother."

THE TREASURE'S WORTH.

OLD Mr. Matthew Money Grub
  Had such heaps of gold ;
He put it here, he poked it there,
Beneath the floor or anywhere.
Once by a moss-grown wall he thought to hide
A sack of crowns : never to walk or ride
Poor Matthew dared, for fear that thieves should come,
And steal his idol, terrible though dumb.

Poor Grub, he scarcely dared to look
  At the fresh posies,
Lest watchful folk might chance to guess
  How, 'neath the blooming roses,
His wealth lay hid.   If near them people linger'd,
He trembled, lest perchance his gold they'd fingered :
For days and months this weary watch went on,
Till one dark morning found the whole store gone !

Yes, that hole was empty quite,
  Vacant as miser's heart ;
Of all the fortune he possessed,
  Vanished the larger part.
He wrung his withered hands in loud despair :
" My gold, my gold, it must, it must be there !"

He peered about, weeping hot tears of rage ;
His sobs brought near a wise man bent with age.

" Can I assist in any way ?
   What is it ails, good friend ?
   Believe, I kindly do intend
To serve you, neighbour, if I may.
What means this hole so deep ? is it a grave ?
Have you some darling lost, that thus you rave ?
                  Some little child, may be, causes
                     these sighs ;
                  Patience, sad heart, not here its
                     spirit lies."

                  But Grub, with haggard eyes,
                  Looked up in wild surmise.
                  "A buried child, a friend, 'twas
                     more—
                  Hid deep, my golden store
                  Was here, safe, as I hoped, from
                     knavish hands ;
                  But see, its hiding-place all empty
                     stands.
                  Oh, I will track the thief, he shall
                     be hung !
                  My crowns, my crowns!" to the
                     cold earth Grub clung.

Kindly the stranger spoke,
  "I pity your distress,
Although its cause might sadder be,
  Yet rouse emotion less;
Arise, and bear your losses like a man,
To find the coins I'll help you all I can ;
Yet, friend, how is it that your gold knaves found,
Where last it should have been, deep in the ground ? "

"Money, that every hour
  So surely comes and goes,
Still passing for a thousand needs
  Besides mere food and clothes,
Meant for our wants and those of others more—
How could you bury it, the precious store,
Which each day must disturb ? " "What's that you say ? "
Cried Grub, " It's been a twelvemonth hid away.

Disturb it ? Never, neighbour !
  Deep, deep in earth
It laid unspent, and might have lain,
  None knowing of its worth.
Clothes, food, on such I waste but little money,
And as to drones, they seldom touch my honey :
I never lent or gave, but let it be ;
Alas, 'tis stolen, miserable me !"

The other, looking at his neighbour
  With scornful wonder deep,
Cried, " What ! was THAT the thing you called sole treasure ?
  For that you rave and weep !
Nay, look not angry, friend, I mean no mocking ;
Rise, do not fret, no longer sit there rocking :
Take my advice, no more your loss you'll rue—
Here are some stones, I'll show you what to do.

" First, mark this hole, I'll pile it to the brim."
  " What then, wise sir ? " asked Grub,

As with impatient glance he watched the scene,
   His trembling hand a-rub.
" Why then I'll cover up the sober store,
And we will leave it." " Well then, sir, what more ? "
" Why then, my friend, go home ; think it's your treasure—
'T is fancy fills a miser's heart with pleasure.

" What more can gold do buried in the ground,
   Like any useless thing ?
Its work on earth all ended, dimmed its brightness,
   Silenced its cheery ring :
Its owner owns it not to give or spend,
The poor it may not aid, or good befriend ;
It can but tempt the weak, so, stranger, own
More virtues lie in yonder harmless stone."

THE TWO SHEEP.

IN a large field all covered over
With daisies, buttercups, and clover,
Horses and cows ranged free together
Through all the pleasant summer weather;
There strayed two sheep, one black as night,
One dressed in fleece of snowy white.

The black sheep was headstrong and wild,
And oft to foolish deeds beguiled
The white one, that would always speed,
Where'er the other chose to lead;
So got in trouble, and when blamed,
Instead of being quite ashamed,
Would toss his head, with saucy burst
Baa out, "The black sheep did it first."

One day a boy, a lazy pate,
Ran through the field, whose rustic gate
He left unlatched; it backwards swung,
And on its hinges loosely hung.

Out rushed black sheep with noisy glee,
Calling, "Here, Snowy, come with me."
And Snowy came without a thought,
But soon experience dearly bought.

For as they both did gaily jog,
They met a huge and savage dog,
That barked and bit and tore their fleece
Before the pair he did release,
And when at last he let them go,
They scarce could stand, they trembled so:
The foolish things but slowly crept
Back to the pastures they had left.

For a few days they staid at home,
In the green field content to roam,
Then Blackie, spying in the fence
A tiny hole, cried, "Let's go hence."
He pushed and nibbled, kicked and tried,
Until the small gap opened wide;
He called for Whitey, once again
Did Whitey follow o'er the plain.

Away they trotted o'er the moor,
A place they ne'er had seen before.
" How fine is liberty, how sweet
The grass we were forbid to eat!"
Cried the black leader, as he brushed
Past tender flowers his light foot crushed;
And Whitey meekly followed on,
Without a thought of right or wrong.

Sudden a cry, a deep abyss,
A heathery-hidden precipice,
Unseen by Blackie till too late;
He stumbled, fell, ah, sad his fate!

Down, down he dashed, and Whitey followed,
Into a chalk-pit deeply hollowed,
Where still he gasped, though at the worst,
"Baa, baa, 'twas Black Sheep came down first."

My moral is, pray learn to trample
On ill advice and bad example;
Don't follow until you are quite
Assured that "Black Sheep's" in the right :
What though his track should seem most fair,
And pleasant blossoms flourish there?
He may to hidden perils lead,
And vanish in the hour of need.

WATCH AND WAIT.

IN the green forest
    I heard an oak sigh,
" I am leafless and hollow,
    Dear world, good-bye."

Whispered a soft breeze
    Passing so near,
" While sweet life is left
    There is use for all here—

" For all things on earth,
    Early or late,
If they only are willing
    To watch and to wait."

Still the oak fretted,
    Fluttered, and cried,
" What use ? I am hollow,
    All hollow inside."

Came by a maiden fair,
    Sweet four years old,
Her bright face, all rosy,
    Crowned with soft gold.

Strayed in the forest
    Through the long day,
Stayed till the sunshine
    Turned to cold grey.

Strayed till the pink cheek
    Faded to white ;
Strayed till the little feet
    Failèd her quite ;

Strayed till the daisies
    Folded to rest,
And each tiny birdie
    Lay still in its nest.

Oh, for a shelter
    Shielding from cold !
One stood all ready,
    A tree bent and old.

Into its hollow heart
  Baby-girl crept,
There, on a bed of leaves,
  Peacefully slept.

Slept in its shadow,
  Shaded from ill,
While the pale moonlight
  Beam'd holy and still.

Slept while the nightingale
  Sang its last song ;
Slept in sweet safety
  All the night long.

With the first dawning
  Mother came nigh,
Grief in her troubled heart,
  Tears in her eye.

"Baby! my baby-girl!
  Lost, lost, I fear!"

Answered a laughing voice,
  " Mother, I'm here!

" Here, in a pretty bed
  Hid in a tree ;
Kind fairies made it
  Ready for me.

" Lined it with mosses
  As though they had known
Mother's wee darling
  Must sleep here alone."

She laid her red lips
  On the oak, brown and dry,
And, kissing it softly,
  Said, " Old tree, good-bye."

The faded leaves fluttered
  With pleasure elate,
"There *is* use for the weakest
  That watch and that wait."

THE LESSONS LEARNT IN YOUTH.

WO tiny linnets in one nest
   Were reared, screened by a mother's breast;
   You might have thought them safe from wrong,
   But, oh! the trouble came ere long.
   A schoolboy stole one chirping thing,
   The other bird, with sudden spring
   Flew off, and ranged for many a day
   In liberty all blithe and gay,
   Bidding its brother come away
And join it in its summer's lay ;
But the poor prisoner in a cage
Fluttered about in harmless rage ;
Its leg was tied with cruel string,
And when athirst, its beak must bring
A little bucket, filled with seed,
Or one with water, at its need :
Its only way to eat and drink
To wind a chain up, link by link ;
A heavy task as you may think.

   Its youth passed by in toil like this,
   Then it escaped—oh, hour of bliss !—
Soon found its brother in the trees,
And there they ranged at joyous ease.
Ah, happy birds !—in woodland gay
They perched and sang for many a
     day,
Merry and free, till that sad time,
When both were caught by treach'rous
     lime.
The one poor linnet struggled, beat
His wings against the sad retreat ;

He starved and pined—his fluttering breath
Too soon was stopped by cruel death.
His brother, taught by early care
Hardships and wrong to patient bear,
Rebelled at first, then tamed his grief,
And in submission found relief,
Raising a sweet yet humble song,
That touched all hearts, and gained ere long
Such pity, none could do him wrong.
One smiling maid that heard his lay
Cried, " Sweetheart, you shall fly away,
I will not prison you a day."
She oped the cage—then laughed to see
The birdie safe on poplar tree—
But sighed to hear how sad the note
That poured from his soft feathery throat.
This was the simple truth he sang,
As wildly sweet his measure rang:
"Oh, brother sweet! oh, Lintie dear!
I would, I would, that thou wert here;
Had thy wild youth known some restraint
Trouble had caused thee less complaint,
Time brought relief, and to this tree
Once more have led us, safe and free;
Fretting has parted us, Lintie and me."

YOUNG BRUIN.

ONCE a man owned a pet—a most amiable bear—
  Though perhaps not a pet for which you, sir, would care;
  He found it a small cub, fat, brown, gentle, and mild,
  And had tended and cared for the poor forest child;
Now it came at a call, licked his hands with delight,
And never attempted to hug or to bite.

While our friend was at work in his garden one day,
Young Bruin came to him, and offered to play:
It rolled at his feet with a good-natured air,
Or frolicked and bounded, now here and now
    there;
And when wearied out he attempted to sleep,
Young Bruin lay by him a kind watch to
    keep.

'Twas a warm afternoon, and the brown bear lay thinking
In a half dreamy state, between sleeping and winking ;
Red roses were filling the air with sweet scent,
And the bees were about, all on honey intent,
Loud gnats fluttered by them, and wasps with sharp stings,
On his owner they settled, these troublesome things.

One, a very big wasp, *would* come down on his nose,
And trouble and worry the good man's repose,
Never heeding how often he turned and he sighed,
Never caring that Bruin to catch at it tried ;
It buzzed and it worried, but still took its place,
And at last seemed to doze on the sleeper's still face.

Thought the bear, "Shall my kind friend, because of a fly,
Be tormented like this ? I can't catch it, not I,
My paws are too clumsy, but crush it I might."
So it rose and moved softly to where, on the right,
Lay a stone—a good big one—of which soon possest,
It stole back to cure its dear master's unrest.

So quickly had bear moved that wasp was still there ;
" Ah ! now, stinging nuisance, you'd better beware !"
A great heavy stone fell, 'twas aimed with such skill,
No doubt that a big ugly wasp it must kill.
"Buzz! buzz!"—it was crushed ; but there, senseless, half dead
Lay master, quite stunned by that knock on the head.

So sometimes our friends, with the best of intentions,
Do more harm than good with their thoughtless inventions.

LEGS AND EYES.

THROUGH the forest tangle
    Roamed a youth quite blind;
Soon he heard a cripple
    Slow limping close behind.
Sighed the blind youth, "I'd rather
    Have eyes, and limp like thee."
"Friend," said the lame, "could I but walk,
    I would not fret to see."

    There they formed a contract,
      Signed it on that day,
    That blind should bear the lame,
      And the lame should guide the way.
        Off they set right joyously
        "Whatever may betide,
          Now I have eyes!" the blind
          youth laughed,
            "I legs," the cripple
             cried.

All that day they journey'd
  A thankful pair, I ween,
Troubles shared are lightened,
  As most folk must have seen.
By eventide they neared a town,
  A rustic bridge they crossed,
There lame man spied a bag of gold
  Amid the brambles tossed.

" Stop ! stay !" he cried, " blind frère,
  A well-filled purse I see,
Stoop gently, I will reach it,
  'Tis most surely meant for me."
" For you ! for us ! that's fair."
  " 'Tis mine, I tell you, brother."
" Why, how can it be yours when we
  Both found it," cried the other.

The twain disputed loud,
  While bright the moonlight grew :
" Wanting my feet you had not come,
  Now, fellow, own that's true."
" Without my eyes you passed it by."
  " Which makes it shares, by right."
Then each to prove his lawful claim
  Began to square and fight.

An awkward sight to watch
  These two dispute the prize,
But while each kicked and fought,
  A third, with legs and eyes,
Ran up to mock the foolish twain,
  Urged on their rage, and worse,
While they were rolling on the ground,
  Galloped off with the purse.

Another tale is told :
  Two foolish men fell out
About an ass they owned ;
  Both had a desperate rout.
A lad who saw the fray
  Stole off with peaceful Ned,
Laughing, " I have a donkey found ;
  They each a broken head."

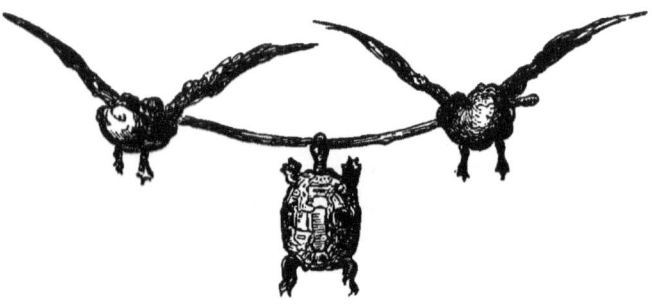

THE AMBITIOUS TORTOISE.

 TORTOISE of a restless mind,
  To travel far felt much inclined,
But in her brown and heavy shell
Was long at home compelled to dwell.

At length two friendly ducks came by :
Poor Mistress Tortoise they did spy,
And heard her wish. With friendly quack,
One tried to lift her on his back,
But, being somewhat thick and round,
Each time she tumbled on the ground.

At length the duck cried, "Fetch a stick,
And she shall travel safe and quick ;

Each one of us can take an end,
If you hold by the middle, friend."
So said, so done, they rose up high,
Half-way between the land and sky.

They bore her safe o'er bush and briar,
These honest ducks, and did not tire.
She might have journeyed all the day
Suspended in this novel way,
Had not a puzzled, wondering crow,
With loudest caws, desired to know
What creature 'twas that travelled so.

"This is the Queen of Tortoise-land,
A mighty lady, very grand,
So think yourself in fine good luck
To meet her," quacked one joking duck.
The tortoise, vain and foolish grown,
The title was most fain to own.

She sudden oped her mouth to cry,
"The Tortoise Queen in truth am I,"
Let go her hold, and instant fell
From the stout stick that bore her well.
And as she fell she gasping cried,
"Say by false vanity I died;
Could I have held my foolish tongue,
I had not thus been downwards flung."

TRIFLES.

WO merchants who the desert crossed
Had on the way a camel lost ;
Loudly with sighs both rent the air,
Their beast of burden was not there.
Then spoke a dervise, holy man,
Lingering to fill his water-can :
" 'Tis sad to see this bitter grief,
And fain were I to give relief.
Tell me, do I your trouble name ?
Is it a camel, one-eyed, lame ? "
" The same," the merchants cried in glee.
" A front tooth gone ? "   " 'Tis he ! 'tis he !"
" Sweet honey on one side he bore,
Of wheat the other held a store."
" Waste no more words, good father, pray —
You've met the beast, lead us his way."
Yet now the dervise did protest
He had but spoken in a jest—
Not having seen the creature ; he
But fancied what its form must be.
The men, enraged, swore o'er and o'er
That he their camel should restore.
A passing cadi all three hail,
The merchants tell their puzzling tale,

"No one, if not of Eblis' tribe,
Could thus an unseen beast describe;
He must have scanned him closely—aye,
Perhaps had stolen him away."
"You hear these men," the cadi said;
"Explain or, dervise, lose your head."
The dervise spoke in grave, calm tone,
"Sir judge, I used my eyes alone;
Long in the desert have I dwelt,
And thrice at Mecca's shrine have knelt,
And unto holy Allah there
Have five times daily raised a prayer;
Have thought, and felt, and dwelled alone,
Holding great nature as my own,
Learning, 'mid wisdom study brings,
To note what men call 'little things.'
Last eve, ere rose the first faint star,
While wandering hither from afar,
I crossed a lonely camel's track,
Left on the sands.   I turned me back,

And marked that all one side—the left—
Was of its herbage quite bereft,
Which showed the creature passing by
Could have possessed but one sound eye ;
Three heavy feet their imprint lent,
The fourth seemed weak, and well nigh spent ;
As to the missing tooth, ah, well,
That was more difficult to tell,
But looking close, a tuft of green
Marking each mouthful could be seen.
The wheat and honey, ants and bees
That clustered still explained with ease :
A fancy picture if it fits,
The magic lay but in my wits.
So now, good merchants, pardon, pray,
If I have caused you to delay :
I had no thought of wrong or ill,
But only bear you, sirs, good will."

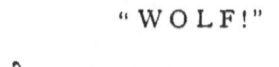

"WOLF!"

YOUNG Colin was a shepherd's
boy,
A shepherd's boy so merry!
His light brown eyes with mis-
chief filled,
His cheeks red as a cherry!
A farmer's flock of straggling lambs
and sheep
From morn till night our rustic had
to keep.

This Colin was a careless lad,
An idle rogue was he—
Just such a one as many a day
In country lanes we see,
Looking as simple as the lambs they lead,
Though not as simple as they look, indeed!

Wild Colin, one hot summer's morn,
Thought he would have some fun,
And raised a loud, excited cry
Which made the reapers run—

"Help! help! fly! hurry! Johnnie, Ned, or Dick,
A wolf is here—a cruel wolf! run, quick!"

    At Colin's cry of "Wolf! a wolf!"
      Pale turned each reaper's face,
    As, catching up fork, rake, or scythe,
      All joined in kindly race.
Breathless arriving, they could only stare,
No savage beast espying anywhere.

    Colin laughed such haste to see,
      And mocked their friendly zeal :
    " Where is the wolf? "—" Sure, I don't know;
      Not this way did he steal.
Neighbours, I only shouted 'Wolf!' in fun,
To see which of you would the quickest run."

    Colin laughed a loud " Ha! ha !"
      As all the men went jogging,
    Declaring that yon lad deserved
      A sound and first-rate flogging.
He laughèd long, he laughèd long and loud
Still mocking at the fast-retreating crowd.

    Colin sat and roared his fill—
      'Twas such a splendid joke,
    That at the thought of each scared face
      Into fresh peals he broke !
Yet others deemed the trick absurd,
When the next day again the cry was heard.

    Our Colin's joke now cost him dear,
      For, 'midst his lambs and sheep,
    A huge grey beast came rushing on,
      Crushing the frightened heap ;
While the young shepherd, in his wild despair,
Cried, "Wolf! help, help!" and tore his curling hair.

Colin in vain for help did call,
  In choking accents, frantic :
" Thank you, sir, no," thought Reaper Dick—
  " We know that silly antic ;
But yester eve you called and made us run—
The wolf that troubles you again is Fun."

Loud Colin shouted, no one came—
  Thinking him but a tease—
While the wolf rushed and ravaged 'mid
  The flock, all at its ease !
The poor boy trembled, and began to weep,
Lest it should eat the shepherd with the sheep !

Colin had lost his voice for dread,
  When Providence befriended :
His master chancing to pass near,
  The tragic scene soon ended—
The creature shot. Our Colin learned that day
It is not safe to call out "Wolf!" in play.

THE PEACOCK AND THE NIGHTINGALE.

A PEACOCK saw a modest, grey-brown bird.
Its eye with friendly admiration lit,
Perched on a hawthorn bush above his head,
    It in and out did flit.
"Off, shabby thing," he cried, with spiteful sneer;
    " Prythee do not come here,
No glittering tail hast thou, or shining wing :
Look upon me, of handsome birds the king,
Then hide thy poor dull head in bush or briar,
For not one passer by will thee admire,
Although crowds gaze at me and never tire."

The brown bird, from its rosy hawthorn spray,
Where spring-time flowers bloomed, 'mid lichens grey,
Trilled all so softly, " True, I cannot boast
    Of shining green and gold,
And no one ever lingers on his way
    My beauty to behold ;
Yet am I well content, for all rejoice
When, as the day declines, I lift my voice,
' The nightingale,' they say, and all attend.
Sir, though your coat is fine, your tones offend,
And all this pert conceit can gain no friend."

THE DIAMOND AND THE GLOW-WORM.

 DIAMOND fell from the jewel fair
That glittered in my lady's hair,
It fell to earth, and none knew where,
    Like drop of dew.

It sparkled all the livelong day,
At night it veiled its 'minished ray,
Until a glow-worm passed that way,
    And chanced to view.

" Art thou the vaunted precious stone
Whose value kings are said to own,
Lying here lustreless, alone ?

" Boast not again thy dazzling light ;
Compared to mine, so twinkling bright,
Thou art, poor gem, a sorry sight.

" Henceforth pray own I am the best
Fit on a monarch's crown to rest."
" Nay," urged the diamond, " cease this jest.

" We from the depths of Indian mine
Are brought, to dazzle and to shine ;
A simple glow-worm's lot is thine.

" Thou hast good use, I do not doubt—
No thing or creature is without.
Thy light may cheer a fairy rout ;

"Or guide poor Puck upon his way,
'Mid dangers, should he chance to stray
While darkening falls the twilight grey;

"Or it may hap, some wandering toad
Or titmouse, lingering on a road,
By thee may track its green abode.

"Such aims be thine, to nature lend
Thine humble services, my friend,
Good wishes on thy work attend;

"But, glow-worm, do not thou compare
Thy light with flash of diamond fair,
Or all will mock conceit so rare.

"It is not in ourselves to know
If dim or bright our lamps may show,
And boasting will not make us glow
    One ray the brighter."

GRANTED WISHES.

WOLVES have a very ugly name,
    Even in friendly fable
  I cannot clear them ; ill names stick—
    To please unable.
Yet here's what happened once : I think you'll say
Wily old Lupus did not have fair play.

Strayed from his closely-hidden lair
    Beneath the fir-trees drear,
Our hungry wolf came lurking late
    A straggling village near ;
He reached a woodman's hut, where, peering, peeping,
He spied a little urchin sobbing, weeping.

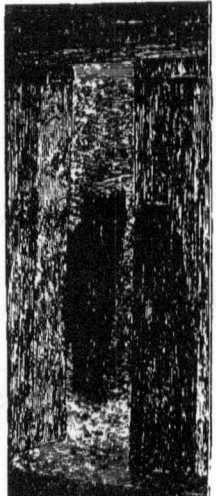

The mother scolding, that her yarn
    Lay tangled, frayed, and torn
By those small hands on mischief bent,
    Busy from morn to morn :
" You're far too ready all things to destroy,
I wish a wolf would fetch you, naughty boy."

Ot course she spoke in angry jest,
    In thoughtless, sudden passion ;
Yet wolf, who heard, said, " Here's a change !
    'Tis a new fashion
To call on us to set such matters straight !
If wolf she wants, *I* must not be too late."

He pushed the door, and walked
    Up to the startled dame,
Who clutched her son, pallid with fear,
    As the intruder came.
" You called me ; here am I, with ready joy.
To carry off your foolish little boy."

Rising, the mother gave a scream,
    A sudden fearful cry ;
Its shrill, wild terror soon alarmed
    A crowd of rustics nigh.
"A wolf ! help, help!" Some
    men came running fast ;
With spring and yell the crea-
    ture darted past.

He hurried to his deep
    dark home,
And breath-
    less crouch-
    ing there,

He sadly mused, " The woman's mad ;
   ' Twas most unjust, unfair
To call me, bid me take her brat, then shout
Because her wish was granted, make a rout ! "

Wolf had to learn that often folk
   Wish senseless, heartless things
While temper rules : all may be thankful
   No magic unkind brings
Fulfilment to such wishes ; should this come
At call, too many of us soon indeed might wish
In truth we had been fast asleep or dumb !

THE HIDDEN WORKER.

A DEWDROP fell on a lily's cup,
  A passing breeze would have caught
    her up :
It thought her so modest, and sweet, and fair,
Too lovely a thing to lie lonely there.
" Come, come on my wings, I can bear thee
    far,
Above the bright world, where such wonders
  · are ;
I can bow the pine-tree, and ruffle the yew,
Yet to gentle beauty be tender and true—
    Sweet scented dewdrop, rise with me,
      away,
    We will float happy, and careless, and
      gay."

The dewdrop clung to her lily bed,
" Oh, not for that was I sent," she said ;
" Oft have I gleamed on the clouds afar,
Bright in the radiance of many a star ;
I have seen the mountain's blue mists below,
I have watched the roses in glory grow,

Till I longed to visit the earth so fair—
Longed for some errand of mercy there.
  My wish was heard, on this flower's breast
  I fell, and here I am fain to rest—

" Rest in patience, unheeded, unknown,
Till my work be given, my task be shown ;
For never, we know, was created thing
But served some purpose of Heaven's high king.
Whene'er I am called, I must ready be,
  Ready and waiting, not floating with thee :
  I choose no path, but content remain
  Until my duty on earth be plain."
    With an angry puff the breeze fluttered loud,
    " Here's a dewdrop thinking herself a cloud !"

It passed away with mocking air.
" Dewdrop," whispered the lily fair,
" Undimmed be thy brightness ; sweet, I see
The angel of flowers hath sent thee to me :
Hide deep in my heart—'tis thy task to give
The scented breath by which lilies live—
The breath that, more than our colours bright,
Fills the heart of man with a pure delight."
  The humble dewdrop, with quick content,
  To the stately lily new sweetness lent—

Sweetness that rose o'er the garden fair,
Bathing in perfume each blossom there ;

Passing away to a sick girl's
        bower,
Soothing the maid in a weary hour
With thoughts of the lilies that
        Jesus loved,
And then of His glory, all lilies
        above ;
Blessing the fragrance, she little
        knew
Its power all lay in one drop of
        dew.

Then floating far, till that fragrance sweet
Reached a lone prisoner's sad retreat ;
Its tender breath in the twilight grey
Like magic chased wrong moods away,
Wafting his thoughts to happier days—
To childhood's home, its simple ways,
Where mother's love his young life blessed,
Where father's hand his young head pressed,
    Where scented lilies bloomed around
    That far-off childhood's happy ground.

The cell, where ever dark shadows cling,
Seemed filled with the breath of some holy thing,

Warming his heart to love and praise,
Chasing the ill of his later days.
Kneeling, at last, with tear-dimmed eye,
Repentant heart, and choking sigh,
He prayed aloud, "Though all defiled,
Yet, Father, Lord, forgive Thy erring child."
　　A hidden dewdrop's silent power
　　Had saved a soul in that dark hour.

BLOW HOT, BLOW COLD.

A TRAVELLER, passing through a wood,
　　In the old days of myth and fable,
Found there a Satyr of jovial mood
　　Standing before a rustic table.

A kind, frank Satyr—pleasant sight!—
　　Who pressed him of his broth to sup;
And he, a tired, hungry wight,
　　Sat down, and took the bowl up.

He blew his fingers, stiff with cold;
　　He blew the broth, so hot and steaming.
"Why do you puff thus?" asked the host,
　　Whose eyes were blue, and round, and gleaming.

"I blow to warm my fingers chilly,
　　I blow to cool my soup so hot."
Up jumped the Satyr in a hurry,
　　And popped the broth back in the pot.

"I tell you, then, Blow Hot, Blow Cold,
　　Out of my cave you go this minute!—
When a man blows two ways at once,
　　One's sure to have some mischief in it."

HASSEYN.

HE left behind the pleasant vale,
   Where grew the palm-tree fair,
Where merchants, resting by the well,
   Forgot their toil and care ;
He left behind the shelt'ring tent,
   The children, swart and brown,
And started o'er the desert drear,
   To reach a distant town ;
But soon uprose a storm of sand,
   The sun burnt fiery red,
To Hasseyn's eyes the track grew dim,
   He trembled, weak with dread :
All famished, fainting, and forlorn,
   He bent his turbaned head.

"Allah is great !" he sudden cried,
   As there before his feet
He saw a bag, one tied with care ;
   " Some meal, some food to eat !"
His trembling fingers open tore
The bag, and low, his eyes before,

Glittered bright pearls, full many a score.
"Pearls, *only* pearls!" Oh, who can paint
His look of horror, he so faint,
The desert drear around him spread.
The simoom threatening o'er his head ;
"And worse," he moaned, with bated breath,
"The vulture's near, I hear its screech,
That tells of slow starvation, death.

"Allah, 'tis true, is ever great,
Yet here He mocks my cruel state :
Would that each pearl had been a bean,
Or dates the poorest eye hath seen ;
Pearls that might ransom proudest khan
Are worthless to a starving man—
These cannot save me, I am lost !"
Far on the ground the gems he tossed,
Then flung himself adown to lie,
Unheeded in the sands to die ;
The treacherous sea of golden sand,
That covered all that desert land.
"Allah but mocks," his parched lips spoke ;
"Allah is good," the echoes broke.

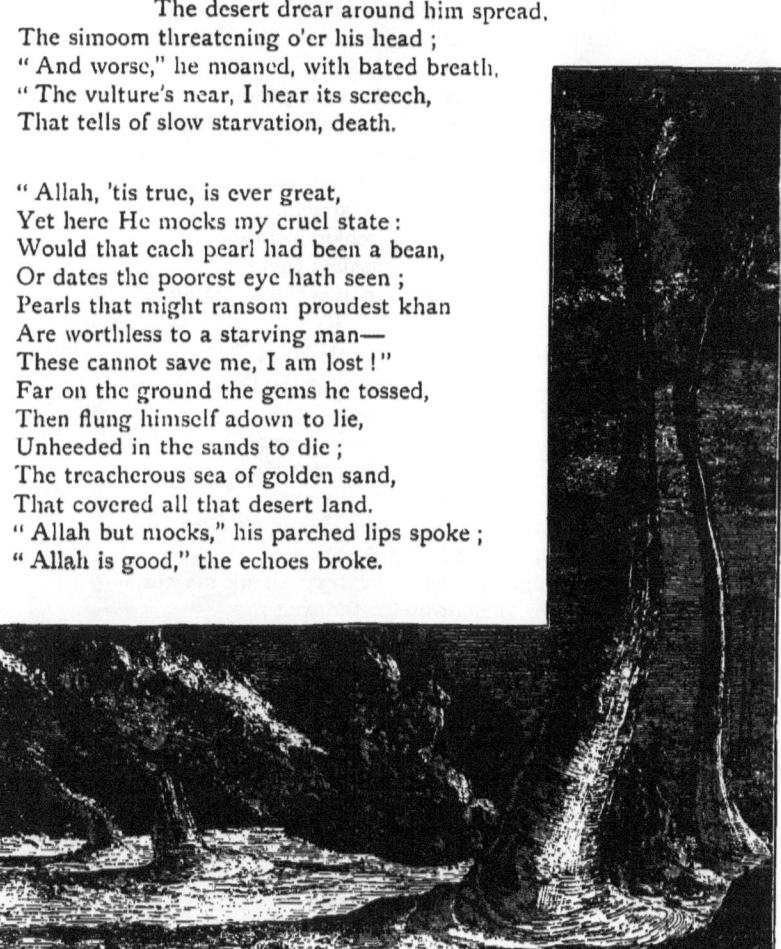

Was it but echo ?   Hasseyn raised
His eyes to heaven, and Allah praised,
For lo, at this his utmost need,
He saw a camel at full speed ;
It hurried on with eager bound,
Bearing a Moor, who, looking round,
Spied his lost pearls upon the ground,
And joyous cried, " My treasure's found !
'Tis open—surely in its fall
The bag hath burst ; yet safe seems all ;"
Then hurried up, with heart elate,
Unconscious of the merchant's state,
Until he found him senseless there,
His arms still crossed in speechless prayer.

He raised him with a gentle hand
From off his bed of scorching sand ;
He laid him on the camel's back,
Safe pillowed by the precious sack ;
He bathed the brow with waters cool,
Brought in a gourd from distant pool ;
And kindly smiled, when Hasseyn's eyes
Met his, in wondering surprise,
And sought to thank.   " Nay, thank me not,
'Twas Allah sent me to the spot ;
'Tis well this lesson we have gained.
His aims with mercy all are rife :
Who could have thought, as each complained,
I lost my pearls to find *your* life."

"A BIRD IN THE HAND."

WITH a stir and a bustle the castle
  resounded—
 To-morrow the Baron would wed;
A banquet preparing to feast the rich
  neighbours,
 And even poor folk would be fed:
The hounds be made merry with savoury bits,
So heard ancient Carlo, half out of his wits.

  The stir and the bustle, and cook in a temper,
   The kitchen no place for a dog—
  One that usually spent all his days by the fire,
   Stretched out like a furry old log;
  To-day he got kicks, and was told to run out—
  He gladly escaped from the noise and the rout.

  Away and away, with a bound and a caper,
   Old Carlo forgot he was lame,

And many a frolic he had in that greenwood,
 And many a limp after game,
Until sudden a huge wolf came up with a bound,
And seized and held fast to the poor trembling hound.

"Oh, spare me for one day, Sir Lupus," he whined.
 Wolf had but just now had his dinner,
So, feeling good-tempered, asked, "Why so, I pray?
 If I wait you will only get thinner."
"Oh no, no indeed, for to-morrow my lord
Gets married, and all our big larder is stored.

"I shall be so well fed that I'm sure to get fat,
 With pullets and pigeons," said Carlo;
"Look, my bones are nigh through, and will eat dry as sticks,
 Just feel for yourself that they are so;
Let me go for this short time, remember the feast,
I will not lose one mouthful," so urged the poor beast.

Sir Lupus considered, the old hound was thin,
 Good fare would improve his condition.
"Will you get all you can, and ere twelve at the door,
 Be waiting and give me admission?
Your paw on the bargain, that you'll not resist;
'Tis a pity that pullets and pigeons be missed."

"I'm a dog of my word; if you'll come to our gate,
 I'll be there to-morrow to meet you;
P'r'aps some pity you'll show!" "Bah!" said Lupus, "no fear,
 I'll be there to-morrow to eat you;
But I'll spare you to-night, if you'll promise and vow
To be ready." "And waiting, as true as bow-wow."

Now the bells have been rung, and the mass has been sung,
 All the feasting is done and over;
The rich and the poor are resting alike—
 E'en the dogs have been all in clover,

And of savoury pieces had such ample store,
Surely never were hounds in such luck before.

But the loud castle clock has just midnight struck—
   That hour for spirits evil and dark—
When wolf sallies forth, with an appetite good.
   "Carlo, old dog, I have come, and mark,
You gave me your word at the side gate to be—
Like a dog of honour—and waiting for me."

"I *am* here," murmured Carlo; "pray, wolf, come in,
   The gate at one push is ready:
You'll just have to pass by a true friend of mine,
   Mr. Bulldog, the porter so steady;
Pray come in and fetch me—he may not bite hard,
Though some call him the chief of the castle yard."

Stout Nero sat blinking by a big kennel door,
   While Carlo stood quite humbly there.
"A bulldog, oh, horrid!" the wolf's eyes glared
   With a frightened, angry stare.
"I've come per agreement to fetch you to-day."
"Well, sir, here I am, ready, so take me, I say.

"I vowed that at twelve I'd be waiting for you,
   And here I am, ready and fat;
I'll not run away, and I will not resist—
   I cannot say fairer than that:
I'm plump as a partridge, and only half waking;
If I am worth eating I'm surely worth taking.

Poor wolf licked his jaws, but glancing at Nero,
   His chest and his ugly big head,
"I wish I had swallowed you thin as a basket,"
   Was all that he angrily said;
"I can do without supper when hard comes the push,
Yet one 'bird in the hand is worth two in the bush.'"

THE PICTURE IN THE POOL.

 NOBLE stag bent o'er a pool
Where waters rippled, calm and cool,
 So fresh and fair ;
No wonder that the shy, wild thing,
 Had lingered there,

Watching its shadow, tall and still,
Reflected in the silvery rill,
 'Mid azure skies :
Its slender form of dappled brown,
 Its tender eyes—

All pictured, 'mid white lilies lying,
'Neath tall green rushes, bending, sighing;
    And watching long,
It wondered at its own wild grace,
    Its antlers strong,

Thinking, " These branching horns of mine
Are all unmatched, and firm, and fine—
    A crown of pride
That I can toss aloft with glee
    On mountain-side.

" But, ah, this body is too light,
These tender limbs are all too slight—
    Would they could change ;
If they but matched my antlered head,
    Safe I might range."

Sudden there rang o'er vale and hill
A sound that roused the echoes still
    That autumn morn—
The sudden baying of the hounds,
    A winding horn.

Swift from the bank our stag in haste
Sprang far across the heathery waste ;
    Its limbs so slight
Bore its fair body safe and far
    From huntsmen's sight.

But stay, its antlers, late so praised,
Caught in a branch, and roughly grazed,
    It held them fast,
Held them until the struggling deer
    Was slain at last.

So is it oft that virtue lies
Hid in the gifts we most despise,
 And what seems best,
Most sweet and pleasant to the view,
 Will bear no test ;

Pleasant, indeed, while all smiles fair,
Failing in time of need and care,
 When only what *is* best
Remains to help us strive for good,
 For peace and rest.

THE PAINTED LION.

 SLEEPING father had a dream,
 A dream so wrought with sadness,
He woke with sob and anguished scream,
 Like one in sudden madness.
A lion's paw uplifted, fell
Upon the son he loved so well,
While, from afar, a warning breath
Cried, "Thus thy boy shall meet his death!"

A dream, an idle, causeless dream ;
Yet all so truthful did it seem,
Peace and content no more he knew,
Faint with distrust his spirit grew:
How could he save his youthful heir
From this dark doom so hard to bear?
He must, he would stern fate deny,
Not thus, not thus his son should die!

The lad, a stripling full of grace,
Was hindered from the wild wood chase,
Close penned within the castle towers,
The fiery youth spent weary hours;
Not his to rise with earliest dawn,
To wake the echoes with his horn;
Not his the forest's wild retreat,
Lest he a lion dread should meet.

One morn, with languid, listless air,
He wandered through the castle fair,
To where some paintings old and grey
Had hidden lain for many a day:
Portraits of mailéd knights so grim,
Portraits of ladies fair and trim,
The picture of a little child,
Another of a lion wild.

A painted lion; at the sight
His eyes filled with an angry light.
" Thou cruel beast! ah, but for thee
A joyous huntsman might I be!
Thou pictured semblance of a thing
That calls itself the forest king,
I fear thee not; 'twas evil hour
A dream hath made me in thy power.

"I would that I could strike as free
At living lion as at thee!"

He struck at paw and flowing mane,
Then wrung his hand in sudden pain;
A broken nail had pierced it deep—
One placed the canvas safe to keep:
Pale grew the fated youth—all saw
Danger linked in this lion's paw.

In wild confusion each one ran
For father, doctor, kindly friend,
Each thinking of that dream of old,
And what it did in truth portend.
Portend, ah, no, but haunting fear
Of danger led to this, 'twas clear.
A few short hours, that nail had done
Its worst—dead was the only son!

'WARE A STRANGER'S ADVICE.

HIS ancient cormorant, grown old and weakly,
  Found it hard work to fish,
And for some easier way to dine
  Began to plan and wish—
Determined, could he find a tool,
To lure into a small deep pool
His prey, so wary as a rule.

A lobster passed—he called out "Hi!"
The lobster anxiously asked "Why?"
"I only wished to say as you went by,
  The master of this lake comes here to-morrow,
  With every net and hook that he can borrow,
  And means to drain it all, the more's the sorrow.

" Then each poor fish that's caught he hopes to send
As present to a relative or friend ;
Some for the market, too, he does intend."
   Off went the lobster in a hurry ;
   This news produced a pretty flurry,
   Seeming, I own, good cause for worry.

The finny tribe, rushing from here and there—
Too frightened now to act with usual care—
All gathered round the bird, with fishy stare,
   And thus they spoke, while loud the splashing grew :
   " Mighty Sir Webfoot, are your tidings true ?
   If so, pray help us—tell us what to do."

" Well," said our cormorant, " 'twere best to range,
And ere to-morrow all your lodgings change.
I know a charming spot, 'tis really strange,
   The coolest pond, my dears, beneath the sun !
   And there, as fast as my long legs can run,
   I'll carry you in safety, every one."

What should they do ? The stranger spoke them fair,
And only for their safety seemed to care ;
No wise one by to bid the fish beware.
   Poor little ones, they trusted this false friend,
   Who but to serve himself did e'er intend,
   As quickly he from lake to pool did wend.

Alas ! they found out, when it was too late,
They were all trapped, food for Sir Greedy Pate,
His six tall young ones, and a hungry mate !
   Our story of a moral need not fail—
   Put not your trust in every stranger's tale,
   Or your simplicity you may bewail.

LEAVE WELL ALONE.

"AH! mistress, Janet Evergreen,
   Ne'er closes ear nor eyes,"
Yawn the two maidens of the farm,
   As at grey dawn they rise.
"Dawn; ah, no, not even so!
   Ere springs the earliest lark,
She rouses us to work and wash,
   While yet the skies are dark.
      'Awake, my girls, 'tis half-past three,
      Hear, the cock crows, unfailing he.'"

"To work, to work," so calls the dame;
Every morning 'tis the same—
They grumble and turn, but, obliged to rise,
Say, while rubbing their sleepy
   eyes,
"Were it not for that cock we
   might get some sleep;
Old Dame Janet would snoring
   keep.
'Tis a troublesome, loud, ill-
   favoured thing—
We wish we could manage its
   neck to wring,
   Nor longer hear its
     'doodle-a-dee,'
   'Get up, my maids,
     'tis half-past three.'"

Next morning strikes, one, two, three, four,
Mistress and maids alike loud snore ;
Five, six, then madam jumps out of bed,
Tearing the nightcap off her head ;
Scolding and fussing, a loud to-do—
" This house is going to ruin and rue,
With idle lasses like mine, I trow."
But they laugh'd to think of the silenced crow—
    No longer its morning song could be,
    " Get up, get up, 'tis half-past three."

'Twas a clever revenge that bird to choke,
Whose noisy call their slumbers broke ;
The bird is silent, but, alack o' me,
There are two sides to each thing, for see—
Dame Janet no longer goes off to bed,
But sits at night in her room instead,
Bringing a light when the clock strikes two :
" You have slumbered enough, there is work to do ;
    Get up, get up, no reason I see,
    Young girls should sleep till half-past three."

ONLY A NAIL.

THE harvest is over, the corn is
    sold,
  Thomas the farmer counts his
    gold ;
He ties it up in a canvas bag,
Then off he goes to saddle his nag.
" I'll away at once to the town,"
    says he,
" Safe in the bank my money to
    see."
  With a clinkity, clinkity, clinkity
    clink,
  How merrily, merrily gold does
    chink !

He saddles his horse, and gets on its back,
When a nail drops out of its shoe : " Good lack !
But I need not stay for so slight a loss,
As I want to trade at the Old Stone Cross ;
For a single nail, that cannot matter,"
So he gallops away with a noisy clatter ;
        While a clinkity, clinkity, clinkity clink,
        His gold does merrily, merrily chink !

When he has ridden but half the way,
The old brown nag is forced to stay ;
For the nail that dropped has loosened his shoe,
And off it flies—a pretty to-do !
Cries Thomas, "Ah, well ! as no forge is near,
I cannot supply its place, I fear !"
        Still a clinkity, clinkity, clinkity clink,
        His gold does slowly, slowly chink !

Only a nail, and only a shoe !
But the road is hard, and flinty too !

Old Dobbin limps slowly now, I trow,
And dark the night begins to grow;
Then the road gets worse, and the rain pours down—
" I wish," said Thomas, " we were in town!
      Too loud does my gold go clinkity-clink;
      I hope no stranger will hear its chink!"

As they ride by a hollow beech-tree,
Out jump robbers, one, two, three!
Thomas springs up on his horse in a flurry,
And does his best the poor beast to hurry;
But how on three shoes can an old nag go
On this rough road, I should like to know!
      Loud on his back sounds the clinkity-clink
      Of gold that makes such a terrible chink!

The robbers soon stop them, and flat on the ground
Poor Farmer Thomas a place has found!
The robbers have flown, and so has his bag—
They have left him alone with his limping nag.
As he leads him home, you may hear him rail,
" What troubles may come from the loss of a nail!
      That only has stopped the gay clinkity-clink
      Just now my gold did merrily chink!"

OLD GAFFER GREY.

" GOOD father, you seem very busy to-day,"
  Said a youth, as he idled along by the way
  That led past the meadow of old Gaffer Grey.

Old Gaffer looked up: " I am planting a tree ;
'Tis as yet but a sapling, and small, as you see ;
Some day, if it prospers, 'twill spread far and free."

" But why trouble to plant it at all ? You are old ;
Such things may take years ere they flourish, I'm told,"
Cried a second young speaker, as thoughtless as bold ;

" For you never may sit 'neath its shadows so long,
Or gather wood-nuts from its branches so strong,
Or e'en list to its leaf-hidden nestlings' song.

"A good grandsire like you must, beyond any measure,
Much prize and enjoy his life's evening leisure:
Why should you now toil, and for other folk's pleasure?"

"My son," asked the old man, again bending low,
"Is there any known age when no service we owe?
When no work's to be done, while on earth we can go?

"That these trembling old hands are but weakly, 'tis true;
Aye, alack, small's the task I am able to do,
And less the result I can e'er hope to view.

"But when even the name of old Gaffer is dead,
This now tiny sapling may raise its green head,
And work some good service in Gaffer's poor stead.

"Your grandchildren's children come dancing around
Its pleasant cool shadows, may frolic and bound,
Or toss its brown acorns that cover the ground.

"And here old folks or sick ones may linger to rest,
Or to muse, as the red sun sinks low in the west,
While the wild birds above twitter hymns in their nest.

"It may shadow the cattle in hot July storm,
Or the ewe with her lambies all dripping-forlorn,
Even shelter a beggar, all weary and worn.

"Sirs, I fancy all this, as I dig with a will,
And feel that a place in God's great world I fill
While I work for my fellows with all my poor skill."

The three young friends departed, but many a day
They told of the lesson they learned on the way
That led past the meadow of old Gaffer Grey.

PUSSY'S ONE TRICK.

ONCE a cat and a fox—most unusual sight—
    Became friends, fed, and frolicked together ;
Whatever the one did the other thought right,
    As they wandered amid the sweet heather.

Said the cat to the fox, in the midst of their play,
    " Shall I teach you a trick, dearest brother ?
You might find it of use should the hounds come your way,
    'Tis the one *I* would try, and no other."

" Oh, thank you, sweet Puss ; pray excuse if I smile ?
    But *one* trick !   Why, I know at least twenty !
All foxes are noted for cunning and wile,
    And of artful recourses have plenty.

" We can run like the wind, can double or back,
    And to puzzle the dogs is our care ;
We can——"   Loud through the wood ran the cry of a pack,
    That had crossed on the track of our pair.

" 'Tis time for your twenty !" cried Pussy ; " be quick.
    I've nine lives to save !" and she ran up a tree ;
Out of sight, out of reach, 'twas her one simple trick,
    But it answered her purpose, for Kitty was free.

Though Foxy did wonders, his cunning and skill
    Availed not to save poor Sir Reynard a rush ;
The turn and the double, and all his fine tricks
    Soon ended—our huntsman can show you his brush.

The moral is simple—if, indeed, we need any—
One good way to an end may be better than many.

HELP ONE ANOTHER.

 POOR little donkey goes stumbling along,
   Weighted down by a load of jugs, baskets, and bags ;
His owner ne'er stops save to give him a blow,
   If poor little helpless brown Neddy but lags.
Soon he meets with a friend—one that owns a fine horse :
As they both go along they fall into discourse,
And while the two masters talk this thing and that,
The steed seems inclined with the donkey to chat.

" How laden you are ! Look at me, I but bear
Light trappings, all made for my own private wear.
Am I not strong and graceful ? " Then said the poor ass,
" Aye, sir, you are handsome—I'm sure none would pass,
And not note your proud beauty. But, oh, if you would
But just help me a little, it would be so good :
These things that outweigh me, you scarcely would know ;
I am weak, and that tired, I scarcely can go.

" My legs ache so badly, they tremble and
    bend :
Oh, help me, fine sir, be a poor donkey's
    friend."
The horse nods his head with a snort and
    a jeer.
" What ! *I* take a donkey's load ! Nay,
    never fear.
What a favour to ask ! what an impudent
    jest !
If you're tired, good Neddy, why, stand
    still and rest."
He kicks up his heels, and tosses his
    head ;
Very soon the ass staggers, drops down,
    and is dead.

Then the cruel taskmaster discovers, too late,
His poor patient slave could not carry the weight.
He storms and he rails, as he lifts pots and jugs,
At overfilled baskets impatiently tugs ;
Then he tries to coax Ned with a handful of clover,
Or fright with a stick ; but Ned's troubles are over.
Blows, threats, and hard words are all tried, but in vain—
That Neddy will never more stir is quite plain.

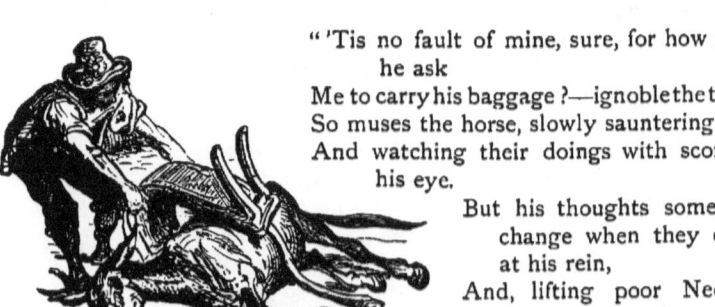

" 'Tis no fault of mine, sure, for how *could*
    he ask
Me to carry his baggage ?—ignoble the task."
So muses the horse, slowly sauntering by,
And watching their doings with scorn in
    his eye.
But his thoughts somewhat
    change when they catch
    at his rein,
And, lifting poor Neddy's
    stiff form from the plain,

Place it up on his back, and secure it quite fast,
Then on the dead donkey its saddle they cast.

'Tis in vain that he shies, and struggles, and kicks—
To the town he must go, guided there by their sticks ;
Both men in a hurry have no time to linger,
While children run out, pointing each idle finger,
Crying loud, " Here's a sight, an ass taking a ride
On a big horse's back ! " Ah, where now is the pride
That made him forget the old saying so true,
" Help others, or some way you surely will rue ? "

THE GOLDEN EGGS.

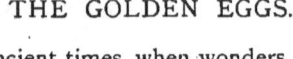

IN ancient times, when wonders were,
    Those famous days of old,
Miles Collins found a fairy hen,
    And she laid eggs of gold.

Miles prospered fast, and soon of wealth
    He would have had great store ;
Each golden egg delighted him
    So much, he longed for more.

One egg a day ; why not obtain
    At once all Henny's treasure ?
Thus, like a miser, Collins lost
    In honest gains his pleasure.

The little bird, so kind to him,
    He watched with evil eye,
And, urged by selfishness and greed,
    Determined she should die.

He thought to find this fairy friend
    With richest treasures filled,
But empty 'neath his cruel knife
    Lay the white hen he killed.

His bird once dead, her eggs no more
    Came golden—one by one.
Miles Collins cried, with broken voice,
    " I'm ruined and undone !

"Oh, neighbours all, bewail with me,
    For I am bankrupt quite."
They came, they saw, but all they thought
    Was, " Serve the miser right ! "

THE FLATTERER.

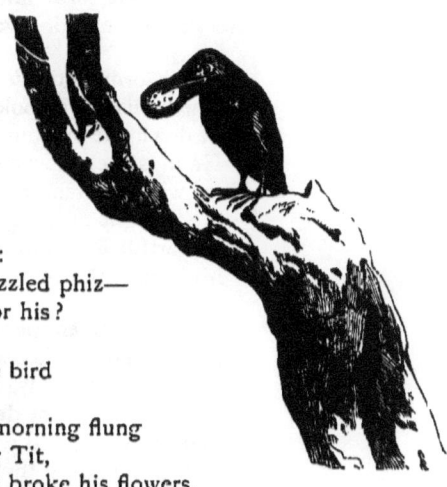

D ON Reynard, in his walks
    one day,
  Passed by a rustic gate,
And in the trunk of an old tree
  A raven saw, elate,
Preparing in its green retreat
To feast upon a piece of meat :
Don Reynard stopped with puzzled phiz—
How could he get that meat for his?

    He knew as little as the bird
      It was a poisoned bit
  The gardener had that morning flung
    To serve out thieving Tit,
  The next door cat, that broke his flowers,
  And did more harm than hailstorm showers.
        " I'll try what flattering words can do
        To win that mutton, friend, from you."

    Such were his thoughts as, bowing low,
      He cried with humble voice,
    "That I have met thee, bird of Jove,
      Allow me to rejoice."
        "What do you mean?" the raven said,
        As he jerked out his huge black head,
        And peered, and perked, and stared about,
        Yet fluttering, as in modest doubt.

    "What do I mean ?   That mighty Jove
      His blackest eagle now has sent
    To bring poor me a dainty meal,
      That I may be content;
    Thee, royal messenger, I greet—
    Pray drop the morsel at my feet.

At thy proud form, and eye of fire,
No wonder mankind gaze and never tire."

"'Proud form, and eye of fire !' How nice!"
  The foolish bird took all for good,
Cast down the mutton in a trice—
  He must act as eagle should.
Then with a harsh and sudden croak
  He thought most royal, off he flew,
While artful Reynard, o'er his meal,
  Muttered, "More goose than eagle you."

The hungry raven, perching near,
  Heard that the fox was mocking plain,
And vowed, now it was all too late,
  Words should not deceive again ;
While Reynard rued with haggard eyes
The meal he lately thought a prize ;
His fair false words had brought him pain,
And well deserved such flatterer's gain.

THE COWARD HARE.

HOULD the tall willow
    rushes stir,
      Loud his heart 'gins beat-
        ing;
Should a partridge sudden whirr,
    Wild he flies retreating.
" Alas!" he pants, " how sad it is
    That I, so harmless, weak,
Must tremble at each forest thing,
    And rest all vainly seek !

"All things I dread, yet none
      dread me,
    But mock me as I bound—
The haunting fear that fills my
      heart,
    For them is only sound.
Dark shadows fall across my path,
    Wild leaflets dance and quiver :
Ah, would my weary life might
      end
    E'en in yon restless river."

Passing, he tastes the tender green
    That springs along his way,
Till tiny woodmouse dances past,
    And startles him in play ;
A squirrel lets his filbert fall,
    While blackbird from a tree
Flings a brown snail that scares
      him so,
    He flies across the lea.

Ears drooping, poor hare sadly
      jogs
    To the pool's rushy brim,
From which out hop a crowd of
      frogs,
    Quite terrified at him,
With splash and croak they
      tumble,
    Headlong out of the water,
'Tis plain each froggie humble,
    Fears that hare may slaughter.

He stares at them in strange sur-
  prise,
  "What, all afraid of me!"
Then sudden feels his courage rise,
  "How! can it really be?"
Had only one frog turned on him,
  He had most basely fled;
But as they hurry off in haste,
  Our hare pursues instead.

He follows fast across the wold
  The frightened timid things;
And as they fly with terror
    cold,
  He loud defiance flings.
"Ha, ha! come back, frogs, if you
    dare,
  And face me; 'twill be seen
By all I am a warrior known,
  The champion of the green."

He chases them all up and
    down,
  Cocking his ears quite bold,

With fiercest airs those frogs
    appals,
  Till out of reach they've rolled,
Thinks himself big because they're
    small,
  And brave, for weak are they,
Yet still at heart a craven thing,
  With which the shadows play.

So is it with all coward knaves,
  Or hare, or man, or boy,
Should chance allow, they do
    their best
  To weaker ones annoy.

THE HATCHET.

AN aged woodman lingering stood
   Scanning a noisy streamlet's dashing,
Where bending willows stooped to kiss
   Their shadows, calm amid the splashing;
Home wending, from its mossy bank
He dropped his hatchet, deep it sank:
A useful tool, though far from new;
The poor old man, what should he do?

A woodland fairy came that way,
   And stopped to ask amid the clatter
(He was a kind, good-tempered fay),
   "Why, friend, whatever is the matter?
Say, have you lost your wits to-day?"
"Oh, no, sir; worse by far—my hatchet;
It lies deep down, I saw it sink,
And I'm too poor to hope to match it."

"Wait," cried the stranger, with elfish laugh,
   As down 'mid the water-lilies fair
He lightly took a sudden header,
   Scattering the tangled leaflets there;

Gliding about in that dark pool,
As though he loved its waters cool;
Diving with more than mortal ease,
Till he the axe could see and seize.

Then up he held it, and cried in glee,
  "Old man, look, I have found your hatchet."
But the good fellow made no sign,
  And never moved one step to catch it.

"That one, kind sir, is shining
  gold,
Mine was of iron, rusty, old;
Had served my father and
  my brother—
No right have I to any other."

The fairy smiled, and dived
  again,
  This time a silver axe he
  brought.

"Now, surely, friend, you are well content
　To own 'tis the very axe I sought."
The honest woodman shook his head,
And turning from the treasure, said,
" Mine was not silver, no, sir, no;
It cost ten groats long years ago."

Again the kindly elf plunged in,
　And tossed a hatchet to the shore;
Bob clapped his hands with simple glee
　His ancient tool to see once more,
Then, having thanked the dripping fay,
Contented, would have gone his way,
But stood surprised, for he was told
To keep the silver and the gold.

" Take your own axe, but take these too,
　And keep them, man of honest feeling;
We fairies have respect and love
　For all straightforward, plain, right dealing:
Truth is most rare that never bends
To play with doubtful, well-meant ends;
Truth is most true when, as its cost,
The things we value most are lost."

PULL TOGETHER.

TWO terriers, Tim and Toby, by one chain
  Were linked in very close communion,
Their only chance of pleasant days
  Lay in a kind and friendly union.
Together if they could agree
They might rove happy, fond, and free,
But many a tug each gave his brother,
For one would ever lead the other.

When Toby trotted off to take a run,
Why, then a tussle instantly begun ;
For if his steps turned to the right,
Then for the left would Timmy fight ;
When Tim to the right inclined,
'Twas leftwards Toby made his mind :
Of course both led a restless, wretched life ;
Who pulls two ways must needs have strife.

This temper was so known, that Spotty cat,
  Although she dreaded dogs like very fire,
Daring these two, stole bones and meat,
  Regardless of their noisy ire ;
For soon that artful Spotty knew
  The foolish pair would not pursue ;
  While she past them would fly—a
    scamper—
  Each would the other terrier hamper.

Once, roaming with the keeper, here
  and there,
    A full-grown rabbit quickly
      darted past ;
  I need not tell that Tim and
    Tobe
    Pursued poor Bunny far
     and fast—

It was the work
each loved to
do ;
But, to their fool-
ish tempers
true,
Instant each
rushed the se-
parate side
Of a huge oak-
tree spreading
wide.

"Come round, come round," barked Tim,
half choking,
" 'Tis yonder hides our rabbit, only
see."
" I shall not follow you," cried Tobe,
" So turn, and hurry after me."
Each one strained with might and main,
But only hurt himself and chain ;
While Bunny reached his home with ease,
The two still struggled 'mid the trees.

The keeper hurried, all enraged
    To find, as often he had found before,
His two dogs struggling here and there,
    No rabbit ready for his store.
He cried, while thrashing with good will,
" I'll teach you to agree ; 'tis ill
For those bound by a chain of any mode
To seek each one to run a different road."

MY WISE PARROT.

"A PARROT, ma'am?" the dealer
    asked;
  "If you'll walk in I'll show you
    many;
'Tis odd if, in such store as mine,
  To please you I cannot find any."

Yes, there were birds of various sorts,
  Green, white, and red, of every size,
Such clambering, screaming, saucy things,
  Filling the warehouse with their cries.

Some birds from India yelled "Poor Poll,"
  And one, a snow-white cockatoo,
Asked me in accents hoarsely mild,
  " My pretty lady, how d'ye do ? "

They talked and shrieked and chatted
    loud ;
  Some laughed, while others called the
    time—
In fact, to tell of all they did
  Would fill my book with jingling
    rhyme.

Nigh deafened, I at length turned back
  To a small cage beside the door.
"Why, here's a silent parrot! Friend,
  Why don't you talk ? " " I think the
    more,"

He answered, with a sidelong look,
   A solemn look that meaning bore,
And shaking oft his handsome head,
   Repeated low, " I think the more."

" This is the bird that I will choose,
   Sir Merchant.   Thank you for a prize ;
I shall hear wisdom by his voice,
   Not merely idle words and cries."

I took him home, my pet admired,
   And longed to hear him wise things say,
But one set speech, " I think the more,"
   Was all he ventured on that day.

'Tis all he said, 'tis all he says,
   With grave calm look and pompous tone ;
That he would sometimes " think " the less,
   And " talk " the more, my wish I own.

A clever thing repeated oft
   Loses its point—that we all know ;
And of what use reflections deep,
   If they no good result can show ?

"DON'T CARE."

"MY son, go not near to the river,
For, dearie, I tremble and shiver
To think of you there.

"All its banks are so muddy and steep,
Its blue waters so clear, yet so deep,
That ill you might fare."

So we hear Johnny's mother one day,
As he sullenly wanders away,
With a mumbled "Don't care.

"I am not a silly, but clever,
And I'll go my own way for ever—
I will, that I swear."

As he strides, the red daisies he crushes,
Then, spying a handful of rushes,
Tall, bending, and rare,

Fast he scampers off down to yon pool,
Where the waters lie rippling and cool,
And lilies float fair.

"I'm no babe, to be told where to go;
I'll soon show her I know that, and so
      Need not her 'beware.'"

What treacherous things are those rushes,
For, as a tall armful he clutches,
      He meets with a scare.

In he tumbles headlong with a souse,
Splashing wild, like a poor choking mouse,
      Eyes wildly a-stare.

He gives a most heartrending cry,
Flings his arms up to willows and sky,
      But neither can bear.

Ah! well he remembers that warning
Just now he was mocking and scorning;
      Scorn's drowning him there.

Yet his fortune is not quite so bad
As to leave the unfortunate lad,
But leads Dr. Evertalk where

He can see his worst scholar, and hear
His loud shouts of distress and of fear;
John begins to despair.

Dr. Evertalk, not in a flurry,
(He never does things in a hurry),
Feels for glasses a pair.

Then he puts them on slowly to look
At the boy sinking fast in the brook,
Gives a solemn stare.

"John Brown, ah, hum, in the water;
Been absent twelve times in one quarter,
Of idleness rare.

"Help you out, well, I will, sir, for once,
Though this wetting one's clothes for a dunce
Is shame, I declare.

"Say, John Brown, did you come here to-day
Just to waste your good school-time in play?
Play's a terrible snare."

So he talks as he seeks a dry place,
Where he snugly his boots to unlace
Begins to prepare.

Poor Johnnie has sunk with one gurgling cry,
When a woman in tears dashes by
With the speed of a hare,

Has rushed in the stream and clutch'd her boy,
Dragged him to land like some lightsome toy—
Half drowned the pair.

The doctor stands composedly nigh,
But the mother springs up with a choking cry
      As the lad lies there.

Starting wild with a terrible dread,
Johnnie, her darling, her son, is dead!
      Her child, her heart's care.

Loud the poor widow weeps and sighs ;
"Speak to me, Johnnie, my lamb!" she cries;
      While, with anxious stare,

Evertalk mutters, "'Tis all for good—
A warning for lads to do as they should,
      And lessons prepare."

Johnnie, arousing to life again,
Meets her fond eyes full of love and pain,
      That he scarce can bear.

Johnnie speaks now, in a broken voice,
Words that her patient heart rejoice,
      For truth sounds there :

" Mother, you've saved me ; ne'er again
Will I do aught that may cause one pain
      To a heart so rare.

"Forgive your child, and he'll seek to do
Whatever may seem most fitting to you,
      Lest worse he may fare.

"And you, good doctor, don't stop to scold
When you find a boy in the water cold—
      'Tis a waste of air.

Advice is best when it comes in season ;
Get folks out of trouble and then talk reason,
      Lest they say ' Don't care.' "

ONLY A GOOSE.

 FARMER'S horse had done his work—
Duty he never tried to shirk—
Then from the haycart's hold let loose,
Went meekly browsing near a goose :
Gander began, with strut and stare,
Itself with Dobbin to compare.

" Horses are awkward ugly things,
Devoid of feathers and of wings,
They but upon the earth can go,
And nothing of its waters know :
We geese are surely at the head
Of beast, and bird, and quadruped.

" For instance, I can skim the lake,
Well nigh a flight across it take ;
Can walk with graceful ease—you see
Strangers turn round to look at me ;
My voice, too, own, good Mr. Dobbin,
Drowns that of common lark or robin."

Quoth Dobbin, who was wise and staid,
" Why need such rude remarks be made ?
If of your own self you must prate,
Need you your neighbours underrate.
Boasting that geese in all excel ?
Now I some other facts could tell.

" You fly, but, I have heard it said,
Soon drop again, like bird of lead ;
You swim upon the waters, true,
Yet ducklings on it mock at you ;
The very walk of which you twaddle
In neighbours' eyes is but a waddle.

" Not one of all the things you name
Can you do well, so fie, for shame !
Don't let your idle tongue run loose—
It only tells us you're a goose :
Self-praise, my friend, goes little way—
'Tis what folks do, not what they say."

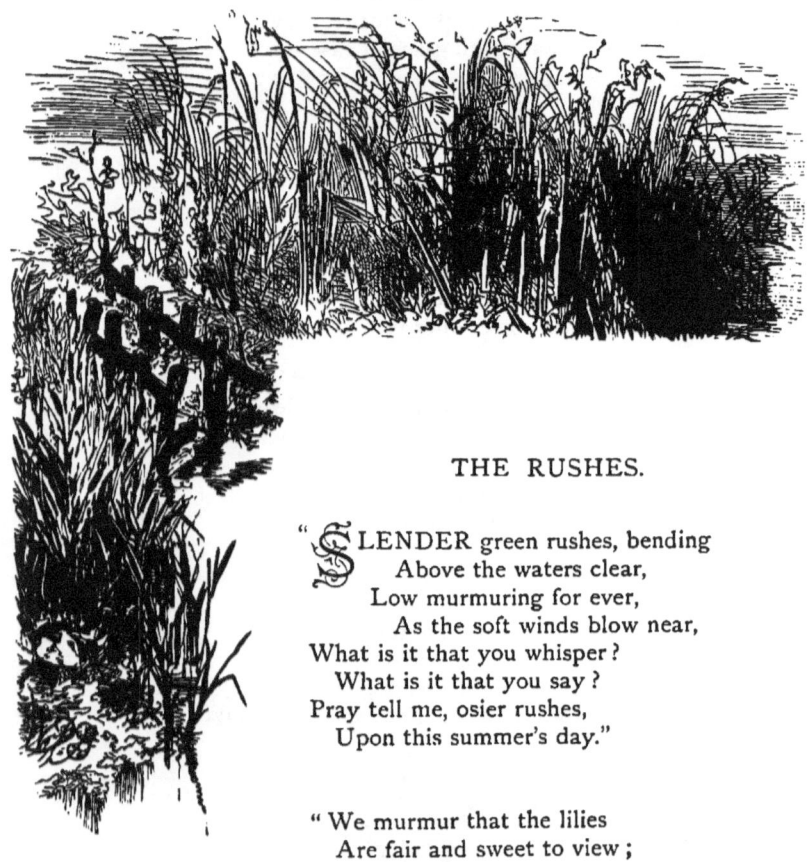

THE RUSHES.

"SLENDER green rushes, bending
    Above the waters clear,
  Low murmuring for ever,
    As the soft winds blow near,
What is it that you whisper?
  What is it that you say?
Pray tell me, osier rushes,
  Upon this summer's day."

" We murmur that the lilies
  Are fair and sweet to view;
We murmur that the river
  Reflects the sky so blue;
We murmur that the birdies
  Can fill the air with song;
While we, poor rushes only,
  May wave the whole day long."

"List to the truth, 'tis very sweet,
   Rushes gently bending,
Proving all have work to do,
   Work to good end tending.
Birds must sing, and flowers must scent,
   The sky beam blue and fair,
For everything upon God's earth
   Has place and duty there."

" Oh ! you, who say that all things
   Have some good work to do,
Must own, we osier rushes
   Prove your fair words untrue;
For here all idly waving,
   And doing naught but grow,
What is the task assigned us,
   We would most gladly know?"

" Osiers form the baskets neat
   Children cram with posies,
Or, to cheer a friend beloved,
   Maidens fill with roses ;
Others hold, all ripe and red,
   Berries warm from shady bed :
Murmuring rushes, is it true
   That no work is left for you?

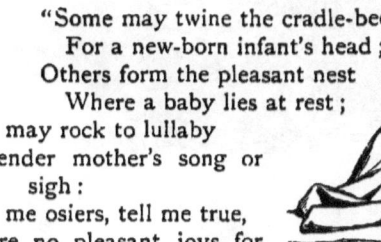

"Some may twine the cradle-bed
   For a new-born infant's head ;
Others form the pleasant nest
   Where a baby lies at rest ;
You may rock to lullaby
   Tender mother's song or
      sigh :
Tell me osiers, tell me true,
   Are no pleasant joys for
      you?

"Need I go on singing, saying
  Of what may be in store,
E'en for willows idly bending
  By the rushy shore.
Prythee, learn the truth I teach,
  Truth for aye unending,
Work and trust are meant for all,
  Grace to fair earth lending."

CASSELL, PETTER, GALPIN & CO., BELLE SAUVAGE WORKS, LONDON, E.C.